Mrs. Henry Wood

Lady Grace

And other Stories - Vol. III

Mrs. Henry Wood

Lady Grace
And other Stories - Vol. III

ISBN/EAN: 9783337122652

Printed in Europe, USA, Canada, Australia, Japan

Cover: Foto ©Andreas Hilbeck / pixelio.de

More available books at **www.hansebooks.com**

LADY GRACE

AND OTHER STORIES

BY

MRS HENRY WOOD

AUTHOR OF 'EAST LYNNE' 'THE CHANNINGS' ETC.

IN THREE VOLUMES

VOL. III.

LONDON

RICHARD BENTLEY & SON, NEW BURLINGTON STREET

Publishers in Ordinary to Her Majesty the Queen

1887

CONTENTS

OF

THE THIRD VOLUME.

———◆◇◆———

A SOLDIER'S CAREER

FROM A RECORD OF THE PAST

VOL. III.   B

II.

It was the following December. Captain Lynn had transferred his quarters to Umballah, where a great portion of the British army was now collected. Preparations were being made for battle, but much uncertainty was experienced regarding the movements of the Sikhs. Some days, news would be brought that they were about to cross the Sutlej; others, that they were crossing it; again, that they were retreating and would not cross at all. But these various details need not be given here.

Captain Lynn, to his most excessive annoyance, had been followed to Umballah by the young Sikh woman, Agee—not to his quarters, of course, but to the town. He had peremptorily enjoined her to remain at Calcutta until his return. The old nurse or attendant, Dayah, had accompanied her thither, and this woman never ceased to urge upon her mistress the expediency of her quitting any place that contained Captain Lynn. One evening she glided into Agee's presence, her face pale, her mouth compressed, and approached with a dread whisper :

'Lady, you *must* leave him now : the hour has come. A few days will see him and his companions mown down ; earth shall hold them no more.'

Agee's lips turned white as marble.

' They are now crossing the Sutlej,' continued the woman in a still lower whisper, as if she feared the very walls would hear her, ' an army of from sixty to a hundred thousand strong. What can their handful of

British troops effect against it?—and that handful not yet conveyed thither?'

'When heard you this?' murmured Agee.

'He came this evening; he is swift and sure of foot, and has outstripped the European news-scouts by some hours; but their great chieftain [1] will know it ere to-morrow's sun be up. He little suspects the fate that is in store for him! They are fine of limb, these northern soldiers, tall and straight; but ere long they must measure their length upon the earth. As the grass falls before the scythe, so must they fall before their fierce and powerful foe.'

'And Captain Lynn?' shivered Agee, from between her bloodless lips.

'He must share the fate of his comrades —what should hinder it? Why, even did you turn apostate to your oath, lady, and

[1] Governor-General.

betray to him what I have now told you, which you know you may not do, it could not serve him, he would still go to battle with the rest. You must escape with me.'

But Agee, with an impatient gesture, turned away and ventured forth into the night. Captain Lynn was leaving his quarters to join a carouse of some of his brother-officers, got up on the spur of the moment, when he came full upon her, stealing up.

'You are on the eve of being ordered out to battle,' she whispered. 'You must not go.'

'Not go?' he exclaimed, wondering what she was talking of.

'Sickness must be your excuse,' she eagerly explained. 'A man unable to rise from his bed cannot be expected to go out to fight.'

' Are you in your right mind, Agee?' he asked, laughing lightly.

'You would never leave the battlefield with life.'

' Then I must die on it, child.'

' You can make a joke even of this!'

' No, not a joke. Though that's a good one of yours about sickness. An English-man does not know what fear is,' he said, drawing himself unconsciously to his full height; 'and for the chances of war, we must all share them, and trust to Provi-dence.'

' Dayah is curious in herbs and medicines,' she persisted, in a despairing whisper, 'many of our women are so. A potion from her would render you incapable of marching with the rest; and to the world you would seem sick unto death.'

' That's quite enough, Agee,' he said, half peevishly, half laughingly. 'You don't understand these things, child. And you promised me yesterday to leave this place! I was in hopes you were gone.'

'You seem strangely anxious to harm my countrymen,' she exclaimed, still reverting to the war.

'Not at all. I wish to my soul they were other than yours, but I must do my duty.'

Thirteen of them were present; the ominous number; and they sat around the convivial table of night. Not with the luxurious appurtenances usual in polished Europe; the rich plate, the glittering crystal, the numerous lights; such things pertain not to a half-civilised land or to a time of war and tumult; but the gay jest, the sparkling remark, and the merry song went round all the same. Gallant, gallant officers they were, true-hearted Englishmen, in the flower of early manhood! And they knew not that the shadow of grim DEATH was upon them, his dart pointed at the heart of *all*.

'The information is so imperfect, so contradictory,' observed Major Challoner, the only grey-headed man at the board : 'if we lance the full tilt of belief into a report one day, it is contradicted the next.'

'In my opinion our march will be useless,' cried handsome Lieutenant Bell. 'I don't believe the Sikhs are coming forward at all.'

'They dare not cross,' burst forth the hot-headed young Irishman, Dan Ennis.

'I hope to goodness they may!' exclaimed little Parker, who had certainly been smuggled into the army, for he was under height, or looked it. 'The glory of routing 'em right and left!'

'They may prove a more formidable

enemy than we think for,' remarked the cautious old Major who had spoken first.

'Not they,' replied Harry Lynn, contemptuously. 'An inorganised rabble never proved formidable. The wine stands with you, Henderson.'

'For my part,' resumed Major Challoner, as he thoughtfully filled his glass, 'I think Sir Henry——'

'Well, Major?' cried one; for the Major had brought his sentence to a standstill.

'What's that in the shade? There! by the entrance? Who's eavesdropping?'

Every head was turned round at the exclamation of Major Challoner. A figure, clad from head to foot in a long black garment, with a cowl drawn over the face, if it had a face; in short, a dim, shapeless form, stood there in the obscurity.

'What do you want? Who are you?'

roared out Major Challoner in his mother tongue; indeed he could speak no other.

'Beware!' was uttered by the figure in Hindostance; a language familiar to some of them only; but the voice was as a strange unearthly sound, ringing with startling distinctness through the depths of the room. 'You sit here, mocking at the Sikhs, but know that the moment you march upon them you are doomed—doomed! They are crossing the Sutlej now, a hundred thousand strong. You will be cut off in your early lives; your fair British homes you will never see again: not one of you but will be struck down; not one will be left alive to mourn the rest! Pray to the Lord for your souls: as sure as that you go out against the Sikhs, your destruction cometh: and they have need of prayer who rush into His presence, uncalled by Him.'

Surprise kept the officers silent. Lieutenant Parker, who had more ready bravery in him than many a man twice his size, was the first to start from his seat and rush after the form; others followed: but it was already gone. They looked outside, and could see no trace of it; but there were many ins and outs of buildings close by that might favour concealment.

'What was it all?' cried Major Challoner, who had not understood a word.

'Oh, a trick of one of the fellows,' said Henderson : 'nothing else.'

'I don't know,' cried the young Irishman, dubiously. 'I hate such tricks. I can fight a host of men hand to hand, and glory in it; but for these ghosts and warnings and omens, I wish the fiend had them all.'

'Did you ever see a ghost, Ennis?' asked Captain Lynn, winking at the rest, for the lieutenant's superstitious tendencies were well known in the regiment. 'What are ghosts like?'

'Which of us was to die, eh?' cried Major Challoner.

'Every one of us,' cried Bell, making a joke of it. 'We had better have a batch of will-making, and go to prayers afterwards.'

'All, eh? That's rather too good a jest,' returned the Major.

'You and all, Major,' nodded Quick-silver Peacock, as he was designated amongst his comrades, from the mercurial tendency he possessed of never being still. 'By George! the black fellow, ghost or no ghost, must think we have tolerable swallows! I should like to get at *his* with my good sword.'

'Thirteen as brave fellows as ever drew breath!' laughed Parker. 'A pretty go if we are to make food forthwith for the vultures!'

'And be sent to our accounts with all our imperfections——'

' If you go on like this, I won't stop with you,' interrupted the young Irishman.

They did go on ; and enjoyed their laugh at him : but there was scarcely one heart, brave though they all were, on which the incident had not struck an uncomfortable feeling, a sort of chill. It was as if they had seen the shadow of Death, which stalked on before.

III.

THE Sikhs advanced unconscious of the mocking disbelief of their British adversaries, and encamped themselves before the gates of Ferozepore, an army sixty thousand strong. That they did not make themselves masters of the town was a matter of astonishment then, and will ever remain such.

By command of the Governor-General, Sir Henry Hardinge, all the troops that could be mustered together at Umballah marched out to meet this force and to succour Ferozepore. They were headed by the Commander-in-Chief, General Sir Hugh Gough, and were accompanied by Sir Henry, who, laying aside his dignity as

Governor of India, took upon himself a command in the army under Sir Hugh. The marches were forced, about thirty miles per day. Both men and officers endured all sorts of hardship and privation without a murmur: the most painful to be borne perhaps was that arising from the want of water, there being none to be found on the route. On December 18, after some days' march, they reached the village of Moodkee about one hour after noon, and proceeded to encamp there, trusting the next day's march would bring them to Ferozepore.

But we civilians, in our peaceful country, talk as we may, cannot form any adequate idea of the hardships undergone by the soldiers in these Indian plains in time of war ; the unconscious British trooper who has never been out of his own island would scarcely believe in them. Long marches in the burning sun, over roads heavy with sand, which, flying to the eyes, goes half-way towards entailing blindness; or trailing painfully through the tangled jungle and brushwood, with no water, no refreshment, to cool their parched lips. We know not what intense thirst is; the cravings of real hunger; the pain of continued and heavy toil. Sometimes, nay often, it happened, through this period of the Sikh war, that when the men had arrived at the end of their march, it would be two hours before the tents and baggage came up, and until they did come there was no chance of refreshment. So the troops, all in a state of physical exhaustion painful to witness, still more painful to bear, would sink down on the ground, utterly prostrated, beneath the burning rays of an Indian sun, or, worse still, under torrents of rain. Was it a matter of surprise that the hospitals were overflowing?

But to return to these men we are speaking of. They arrived at Moodkee, exhausted with their march and with physical privations, and had barely taken up their station before its walls, when the Sikhs bore down upon them and opened a tremendous fire. But weary and unfit for contest as they were, the men had the spirit of Britons, and rushed forward to meet their powerful enemy. They repulsed and routed them for the time, but with a fearful loss both of men and officers.

They were burying their dead the next day, calling over the muster-rolls, succouring the wounded, and consoling the dying, when Captain Lynn and little Parker ran against Lieutenant Ennis.

' I say!' cried the Irishman, 'it's beginning to work itself out. We were thirteen, you know, that night at Umballah, and five are already gone.'

'Four,' responded Harry Lynn.

'Wrong, Captain, they have just found poor Henderson.'

'Dead?'

'Stark and cold. He was under a heap of slain.'

On the 21st the army marched out of camp, leaving it standing, and neared Ferozepore, after a march of sixteen miles. Here they met with General Sir John Littler, commanding about five thousand men. The Sikhs were at hand, and the whole body of our troops were at once formed into four divisions and arranged in fighting order. But again, as in the recent battle of Moodkee, were the unfortunate men hurried into action unfit for the contest, hungry, thirsty, and weary.

The battle of Ferozeshah, as it was

called, began under a mutual assault of cannon ; but the light artillery of the British was of little avail against the heavy guns of the Sikhs, so the firing was ordered to cease and the infantry to advance. The Sikh army was strongly entrenched among the jungle and brushwood, rendering the approach of our infantry not only difficult but dangerous. They advanced in line, and charged with the bayonet, but the firing of the enemy was redoubled: *and the Sikhs had laid mines, which were now fired underneath our soldiers' feet.* Hundreds were thus shattered to pieces ; officers, men, and horses were indiscriminately blown up. The action soon raged fearfully, the slaughter being terrible ; the heavy cannonade of the Sikhs kept up a continuous roar, overwhelming with destruction the ill-fated Europeans : but the latter were gallant fellows, cheering on each other with their

indomitable breasts of valour, carrying much
and overcoming much. The atmosphere
seemed alive with bullets; the roll of the
musketry grew deeper and deeper; the
shouts and noise of the combatants increased
the confusion; above the roar of the tempest
would be heard the voices of the commanding officers: 'Men of the —— Europeans,
prepare to charge. Charge!' and, mingling
painfully with the tumult, rose the shrieks
of the wounded and the groans of the dying.

Night put a stop to the slaughter. Some
of the troops retired to bivouac at a little
distance, but considerable numbers of each
contending party intermingled on the plain
together.

But oh! what a night it was! The air
cutting cold; no tents, no covering, no food
for the exhausted soldiery, who had been
sixteen hours under arms, and, worse than
all, *no water!* Many a wounded man died

that night for want of it. There was very
little medical assistance, for the numbers
wounded were too great to allow of much,
and the shades of darkness were upon the
earth. And so there they lay, poor fellows,
groaning in their agony; no linen to band-
age up their wounds, no pillow to lay their
beating heads upon, save the dead bodies
that crowded there and the horses that
were slain. It was a ghastly sight, that
field of battle, as seen by the glimmering of
some solitary torch; it would be more
ghastly still in the coming moonlight. The
forms of the dead lay stiffened and rigid as
they had fallen, the sharp expression of
anguish yet conspicuous on the livid, up-
turned faces. Officers and men, Sikhs and
British, had fallen there together, peaceful
towards each other in death, though they
were not so in life. Ah! they were equal
now: the officers, some perchance of noble

family, who had been reared luxuriously, and the men, who, it may be, had never known a home, or an asylum worthy the name of one. The one class had received no more care than the other in dying: there was no wife or mother to soothe their agonies of body, no priest to administer calmness to the soul: equal as they would be in the next world, so had been the last scene of their lives in this. But striking more painfully still upon the heart of the beholder, himself hitherto spared, came the incessant cries of the departing—of those who *might* have been saved; the vain cry that went up around for WATER; and the anguished, unanswered calls for assistance, the sharp, eager question of were they to be left there, among the dead, to die!

In a part of the field, near to the camp of the Governor-General, reclining on the ground in their arms, was a group of officers.

When you last saw some of these it was at that convivial night-meeting at Umballah. *All* were not there of that thirteen : five had been slain at Moodkee and three more in that day's carnage. Leaving five : but two of those five were wounded, it was thought mortally.

'I say!' cried Lieutenant Bell, who had been nursed in blue and silver at his mother's apron-string, and had never known a care in the world, except that of his handsome face, 'we were all calling out for a taste of the battlefield, but I don't admire such rough work as this.'

'Rough enough,' commented Major Challoner. 'But there's the glory, you know, Bell.'

'Egad, I'd rather have another sort of glory, than what's to be got fighting with these demons of Sikhs. If they were but an honourable, open foe, meeting you hand to hand, it would be something like. Who would have laid a powder-magazine under our feet, to blow us up wholesale, save these sneaking cowards of heathens?'

'All stratagems are fair in war, they say.'

'Stratagems be shot!' muttered the lieutenant wrathfully. 'I think those prolific-brained enthusiasts who rave so much of the glories of war, Major, exciting one on to become soldiers, might put in a little about its horrors. What was that cry?'

'Only a death-shriek,' said Major Challoner.

'Ugh!' shivered the young man, 'How ghastly the heaps of slain look in the moonlight!'

'Why, yes,' cried the Major. 'One who faints at the sight of blood had best go away from a field when the battle's over. I freely admit that it wants the excitement of engagement to keep one's spirit above zero.'

'Do you know,' resumed the lieutenant, 'the scene has several times to-day put me in mind of a war-description of Byron's? It's in a short poem, or fragment, of his, called "The Devil's Drive." Do you know it?'

'Not I,' growled Major Challoner, 'poetry's not in my line: never read a verse in my life. It may be in yours.'

'It is a glance at the battle of Leipsic. He watches the red blood running in such streams from the mountains of slain, that the field "looks like the waves of Hell." The "he" being the Devil, you know.'

'Ah,' cried the Major, 'very likely. It partakes more of the Devil's work than angels'.'

'Hark at the moans of those poor

wretches, dying for water! Ugh!' shivered the young man again, 'how damp it is!'

'And bitter cold. Lynn, how are you?'

A groan was the only answer Major Challoner received. Captain Lynn had been dangerously wounded in the leg with grape-shot.

'How's the pain?'

'Oh, don't talk about the pain,' murmured poor Harry Lynn. 'If I could only have some water!' Hundreds echoed the cry that night, in vain.

Major Challoner moved away on a work of succour. Exhausted though he might be, and necessary as repose was to him, he could not hear those wails for help around and lie down to his own rest. There came up to the spot soon afterwards, making his way over the prostrate bodies, the young Irish-man, Ennis.

'Lynn! Bell!' he cried eagerly, 'by all that's true, I have seen it again!'

'Seen what?' asked Captain Lynn, rousing himself momentarily from his agony.

'That bird of ill-omen: the black form —ghost, banshee, or whatever it might be— which appeared to us that night at Umballah.'

'Don't be a fool,' retorted Bell savagely, disturbed out of the sleep into which he was falling. 'Your superstitious absurdities are not wanted to-night, Ennis; we've horrors enough without them.'

'I swear I saw it! I swear it by the Blessed Virgin! The same black, shapeless figure. It's dodging about the field, as if it were seeking something amongst the dead.'

'I wish you were dodging amongst the dead!' growled the handsome lieutenant. 'Why did you not stop in Ireland along with your banshees if you are so fond of them? Your teeth are chattering now.'

'With cold,' answered Ennis hastily. 'But I must go back: I am on the Staff, in the place of poor Bellassis. Lynn, can I change your position before I go?'

Towards the hour of midnight, Captain Lynn, between his paroxysms of pain, had dropped into an uneasy doze, when some movement aroused him. The dark shape, spoken of by Lieutenant Ennis, was bending over him.

Doubting if he were awake, or whether it was not a delusion of the imagination, caused by the conversation of his brother-officers, he rubbed his eyes and gazed up at it, when the figure threw back the dark cowl and disclosed to his astonished sight the features of the young Asiatic.

'Good heavens, Agee! What brought—how came you here?'

'I told you I would share your fate, whatever it might be,' she whispered. '*You* talked of separation, and I let you talk, keeping to my own resolve. I assumed this disguise that night at Umballah, hoping to frighten you from marching against the Sikhs. And when I found it was useless, and you left, I followed in the track of the regiment; but I could not come up with it until this night.'

'It was not your voice that spoke to us that night at Umballah!' exclaimed Captain Lynn, bewildered with her words.

'It was my voice, but I spoke through a small bone instrument, in use among the Sikhs, something like a ring; so that none could recognise it to be the voice of a woman. I have come now to save you. I will find you a sure asylum amongst my countrymen. Rise, and follow me.'

'I shall never rise again,' was his reply. 'I am severely wounded.'

'Wounded!' she uttered, in an accent of deep horror. 'But you must not stay in this spot: it is certain destruction.'

'Destruction anywhere for me. Why in this spot more than in another?'

'I have wandered amongst the Sikhs unmolested this night,' she whispered, 'speaking my own tongue. They have just found out the place where your chiefs are encamped, and are hastening back to fire on it. This is in the direct line. You must not remain here.'

'To fire on the camp!' he screamed. 'Bell!'

But the young lieutenant slept heavily. 'Bell! Bell!' continued Captain Lynn.

'What are you about to do?' cried Agee wildly. 'Would you betray me—what I have told you?'

'Betray *you*! No, no, I don't mean that. Sink down here by my side, Agee; the light does not give here, in the shade of the hillock.'

He pulled her down with one hand, and managed, though he could not stir his maimed leg, to stretch out the other till it touched the lieutenant, who partially aroused himself.

'Bell! Bell! fly to the camp. The enemy are upon them, opening their guns. Bell, I say!'

'What guns?' cried the sleepy lieutenant, raising himself into a sitting posture. 'Guns! Where are our scouts and sentinels then? Have we none out?'

'Are you a coward?' reiterated Captain Lynn; 'every moment that you waste is worth a Jew's ransom. Fly for your life, and arouse the Staff. Would you have the camp destroyed?'

The lieutenant, fully aroused now to the sense of the words, started up in haste to do his mission. Captain Lynn turned to that dark figure by his side.

'Now, Agee! quick! you can make your escape.'

'As I have clung to thee in life, so will I in death,' she murmured. 'What, think you, will existence be for me henceforth, that you should wish me to remain in it?'

'This is madness!' he exclaimed in much excitement. 'Agee——!'

Boom!—boom!—boom! rolled the thunder of the Sikhs' heavy gun. It had commenced its work of destruction. Captain Lynn, supporting himself on his elbow as he best could, turned his head to look after his messenger. Even in that very moment, as he gazed, a shot overtook the young lieutenant. With a wild, piercing cry, that reached and rung in the ear of Captain

Lynn, he leaped some feet into the air. It was the last cry that ever came from poor William Bell. He was shot right through the heart.

Captain Lynn, amidst all the smoke and the dismay and the confusion that now reigned around, was conscious of a start and a moan beside him : but not for a few minutes was he aware that the unhappy young lady who lay there had received her death wound.

'Oh, Agee! this is fearful!' he cried, almost beside himself with horror. 'And I am helpless—helpless!' he despairingly wailed, wildly throwing his arms up, in vain efforts to move ; 'I cannot bear you hence to safety and to succour!'

'There is no succour for me,' she returned in hollow tones, 'my soul is flee-ing. But oh, Henry! which dost thou think is more welcome to me—to live on in per-petual dread that thou wilt desert me for another, or to sink quietly to death thus by thy side?'

The camp, so startlingly aroused from its temporary security, sallied out against the Sikhs, but not until fearful havoc had been committed. The whole of the Staff, with the exception of Captain Hardinge, were killed or disabled. Sir Henry ordered her Majesty's 80th Foot and the 1st European Light Infantry to the attack, who drove back the enemy and spiked their gun.

What were the reflections of Captain Lynn as he lay there through the night, with the dead body of the young girl resting against him? Not such as can tend to soothe the conscience of a dying man. He felt that the career bestowed on him from above was over, and how had he worked it out? He saw things clearly now : the near approach of death dashed away the scales from his eyes, and denuded his conscience of its worldly sophistries. The recollection of the life he had led came pressing on his brain. He knew that it was not one that fitted him to stand at that Judgment-bar whither he was hastening, to which *her* spirit had already flown: and, it may be, in those closing hours, in his soul's sharp tribulation, that he wailed forth an agonised petition for renewed days, like unto one we read of— not that he might return to his years of vanity, but that he might strive to redeem the past. But no: the sun went not back for him.

With daylight the battle was renewed. The conflict raged with redoubled fury, and the slaughter on both sides was great. Victory appeared at length to favour the British, and the engagement, it was thought, was over. Our troops began to collect their wounded and bury their dead, when, suddenly, a force of the enemy, thirty thousand strong, consisting of cavalry and their camel-corps with swivels, bore down upon them. The infantry drove them back at the point of the bayonet, amidst showers of round and grape. The British forces were certainly at this moment in a critical position : *all their ammunition was expended, and they had not a single gun wherewith to answer the enemy.* Thirty thousand fresh troops and a heavy cannonade brought to bear upon our ex-hausted and, as far as artillery went, defence-less soldiers ! Yet strange to say, at sight of some threatening manœuvres, the Sikhs fled, leaving the British in possession of the field and of much of their artillery ! And thus, in this strange manner, ended the sanguinary battle of Ferozeshah. You don't want to hear of many such, do you ?

'A well ! a well !' broke forth, in shouts of exultation, from some hundreds of British voices soon after the fighting was over. It was really true : they had discovered one in front of the village they had taken. Bitter disappointment! the water was putrid, it having been half filled with their dead by the Sikhs. Nevertheless, it was greedily partaken of : general officers, poor soldiers, all pressed round to drink. 'Horrible!' shudders the dandy, sipping his claret at home. It *was* horrible ; but when you, my dear sir, shall have experienced the blessings of a forced march under an Indian sun, winding up with a hot engagement of some six-and-twenty hours at its end, without a drop of moisture having gone into your parched lips, you will not turn away from even putrid water.

Two only remained out of the thirteen officers of Umballah memory, Captain Lynn and the young Irishman, and they were wounded unto death. Major Challoner and Captain Peacock had that day fallen. The

Asiatic girl, when she pretended to foretell
their doom, knowing nothing of it, gave a
pretty good guess at the extent of the carnage. They, the two yet living, had been
drawn aside from the dead, and were lying
close to each other, amidst a whole crowd of
wounded; and the agony of their wounds
was even as nothing compared with that
arising from their distressing thirst.

'Lynn,' cried the Irishman, who retained
his superstition to the last, 'we can sympa-
thise with Dives now, when he asks for
Lazarus to dip the tip of his finger in water
and come and cool his tongue. It has been
an unlucky fight for us: there was no es-
caping our fate.'

'We have earned laurels, you know,'
returned Captain Lynn, with half-mocking
bitterness on his lip. Poor Harry Lynn!
take it for all in all, his was a cruel fate, and
his heart was full.

'And lost life,' retorted Ennis. 'For my part, I *expected* the bullet that struck me, after what I saw yesterday. You matter-of-fact Anglicans don't stoop to believe in death-warnings. Perhaps I may see it again before I die : but it must make haste.'

A paler shade, if that could be, came over the face of Captain Lynn, and he pressed his hands upon his temples. He was about to speak, about to tell Ennis that he need have no fear of seeing ' it ' again, when a wild shouting noise in the distance stopped his words.

'What's all that?' inquired Lieutenant Ennis of a soldier who approached carrying something in his hand. It was a man belonging to Captain Lynn's corps.

'We have been rummaging over the Sikh entrenchment, sir,' was the reply, ' and in it we have found the mess stores which they had captured, intended for the Bengal

Native Infantry. There was a lot of beer in it—so glorious! It is being dealt out, and I have brought you some.'

The officers raised their earnest eyes, their parched, eager lips, and a rush of joy, almost frantic in its excess, illumined their dying features.

'God be thanked!—He is with us still, Lynn,' reverently spoke Ennis as he fell back, after drinking of the sweetest draught he had ever yet tasted. 'We can now die in peace. God be thanked!'

'Amen,' responded Harry Lynn.

THE
SURGEON'S DAUGHTERS

I.

LOVE.

Do you happen to be acquainted with the Faithful City of Worcester?—The loyal city which, in its trueheartedness, remained firm to its unhappy king, Charles the Martyr, with his son, when all other of his towns had turned against him, and so earned the right to be called Faithful for ever? If a stranger, you cannot do better than pay a day's visit to it: you may go to many a town less worth seeing. Whilst your dinner is preparing at the Star and Garter—at which dinner you must beg the host not to forget the Severn salmon, and the far-famed lampreys, fatal in his day to the First Henry—go on a tour

of inspection through the city. Take its
cathedral first: and when you have looked
at its renovated grandeur ; at its cold, handsome monuments, erected to the memory of
those who have long been colder than they
are, and admired its beauteous east window
of many colours, step into the cloisters,
where the irreverent Cromwell stabled his
horses, and there pause awhile over the
gravestone bearing the solitary inscription
' Miserrimus,' and speculate upon its unhappy tenant's life and fate. Then, passing through the 'Green,' and the gate of
Edgar Tower, turn to Chamberlain's China
Factory—it has passed into other hands
now, but the name still clings to it, and
will cling, whilst present generations shall
exist. The Worcester china is spoken
of all over the world, and deserves its
reputation: in point of art and refined
beauty it yields to none. You may have

been all the way to Pekin, and bought up
all its curious teacups and saucers; you
may be at home in all the splendours of all
the departments of the Sèvres Porcelaine;
but you see they cannot surpass, if they
can vie with, that produced at Worcester.
Turning about again, from the China-works,
to stand in front of the Guildhall, you
admire its façade, its statues, and its conspicuous motto, 'Floreat Semper Fidelis
Civitas.' Did you ever hear the anecdote
connected with its body-corporate of other
days, when George the Third was king?
His Majesty visited the Faithful City, staying
in it a few days: and this most loyal corpo-
ration exercised their brains devising ways
and means of showing their fealty: as,
between ourselves, corporations do still:
which, it is said, were well and duly appre-
ciated. When the addressing, and the
feasting, and all the rest of it was over, and

the King was preparing to leave the town,
one last and final attention was projected by
the body-corporate. A deputation of them
waited on their august guest, obtained an
audience, and solicited 'the honor of escort-
ing his Majesty to the gallows.' The King
stared, laughed, and thought he would rather
be excused. They had omitted to explain
that they merely wished to pay his Majesty
the respect of attending him out of the town
as far as the spot where the gallows for the
condemned criminals stood. It was at the
top of Red Hill. The King gave permission
to *that*.

The inhabitants of Worcester are said to
deserve the initials P. P. P. affixed to their
names, denoting Poor, Proud, and Pretty.
Whether, take them as a whole, they are
poor, I cannot say; proud they undoubtedly
are, for that is the characteristic of all
cathedral towns; and you certainly cannot

walk through the city without being struck with the remarkably pretty faces of the girls you meet.

At a long-past period, so long that elderly people can only just remember it, there lived in Worcester a surgeon and general practitioner, Mr. George Juniper. He was a little man, with a fair complexion and curly light hair; skilful, kind-hearted, sensible, and much esteemed by his fellow-citizens. He had been in practice many years and his connection was extensive; but he was no longer young, and began to feel the need of a little rest and less responsibility. Mr. Juniper always kept a qualified assistant who was generally a young man; though latterly he had not been fortunate in respect to his assistants. One of them sent a patient poison in mistake for Epsom salts, which nearly cost the lady her life; another grew fonder of the billiard-table than he was of

the surgery; and a third made love too con-
spicuously to the surgeon's daughters. So
that of assistants Mr. Juniper grew weary,
and thought he must try some other system
of help.

George Juniper rejoiced in seven daughters. 'Seven daughters!' cries the aghast
old bachelor, reading this through his
spectacles; 'was he mad?' Well, sometimes
they did nearly enough to drive him so, had
he been less good-humoured and indulgent.
But he could not lay the claim of paternity to
all the seven. It had happened in this way:

There resided in Worcester, again many
years back even from this, an old gentleman
of the name of Battlebridge. He had made
a large fortune in business, and had retired to
enjoy it, or a portion of it, in a great square
handsome house with a large garden, keeping a cook, housemaid, and gardener, the
two latter being man and wife.

Up to one-and-seventy years of age Mr. Battlebridge had not married ; consequently, his dear relatives, even to the twentieth cousin, although they were all well off, were excessively attentive and affectionate towards him, calling upon him and carrying him presents of jam and flannel nightcaps a great deal oftener than he wanted them. But one day it was disclosed to the old gentleman that a graceless nephew of his had avowed, the previous night, in a mixed society, that not one of them 'cared a rap for the old man ; all they wanted was that he should betake himself off, so that they might inherit his gold.'

Whilst Mr. Battlebridge was digesting this agreeable news, there burst into his parlour his cook and housekeeper, Molly ; her cheeks crimson, and her voice angry. She had been having another breeze with the gardener and his wife, such breezes being

pretty common, and had come to give warning. Now Molly was a superior young
woman and a good girl, who looked after her
master's comforts, and old Battlebridge would
as soon have lost his right hand.

'It's two to one,' cried Molly, turning
her comely face to her master. 'What
chance have I against them? They are
always on at me: and Mark is the most
overbearing man alive. If you don't like to
pay me my wages, sir, and let me be off this
day, I'll leave without them.'

'I'll make it two to two for you, Molly,
if you will, and then you can have fair play,'
responded the old gentleman.

'How will you do that, master?'
asked Molly, her passion a little abating,
and her pretty mouth breaking into a
smile.

'Why, I'll marry you myself,' returned
old Battlebridge.

'I am not in a humour to be joked with,' retorted Molly, becoming wrathful again. 'Do you please to pay me, sir, or not?'

'I am not joking,' he replied. 'I'll get the license to-day and marry you to-morrow.'

And old Battlebridge did so: and from that time Molly sat in the parlour with him, and became as much of a lady as she could, and was Mrs. Battlebridge. Worcester made a great commotion at the news; the relatives made a greater. 'Married, indeed, when he ought to have died!' they cried; and they declared that, had they known of it beforehand, they would have shut him up in the madhouse at Droitwich.

Three little girls were born to old Battlebridge, and then he died, leaving his whole property to his wife and children. The relations threw it into Chancery, like the simpletons they were, for they had not a leg to

stand upon. One of them acknowledged that
they had done it in a moment of exasperation : and exasperation, mind you, has been
more productive to Chancery than any other
passion. The money came out of it just
halved in value, thanks to the case being
minus the said leg : had it possessed but the
shadow of one, it would never have come
out at all. But there was a great deal still
left; quite enough to tempt many a suitor
to pay court to the comely Widow Battlebridge. The successful one was Surgeon
Juniper; and the Faithful City wondered.
It wondered that he, being a gentleman in
mind and manners, should take to himself a
vulgar wife : but the surgeon, without so
much as a wry face, gulped down the pill for
the sake of the gilt that covered it.

That the new Mrs. Juniper was in a
degree vulgar, no one could deny : she was
growing plump ; she had not abandoned her

homely speech and grammar, and had not tried
to do so : but she possessed many redeeming
qualities. She was gentle-tempered, kind-
hearted, benevolent to the poor, an excellent
wife, mistress, and mother ; and many a well-
born lady in the city was glad to shake
hands with her and to pay her the respect
she deserved. At the time of Mr. Juniper's
marriage with her he was a widower and
the father of three little girls ; her three little
damsels made six ; and one, who was born
after the double second marriage of the
parties, made the seventh. So that is how
Mr. Juniper counted his daughters.

The little girls grew up in course of time
to be young women, well-educated and lady-
like, but full of fun amidst themselves. Two
of them—the eldest in each family—soon
married ; Ann Juniper to a merchant in
Liverpool ; Mary Battlebridge to a gentleman farmer in Worcestershire.

It was about this time that the following advertisement appeared in the *Worcester Journal* and also in the *Times*: such advertisements being less common in those days than they are in these:

'To the Medical Profession.—A gentleman fully qualified as surgeon, &c., possessing money to purchase a share in a practice, may hear of something desirable by applying to G. J., Post Office, Worcester.'

The advertisement was Mr. Juniper's. He received sundry answers to it, and concluded a negotiation.

Mr. Juniper's house, large and commodious, stood in one of the principal streets. Entering from its pillared portico, rooms opened on each hand: the dining-room on the right, the parlour on the left; the drawing-room was above. All these rooms faced

the street. Mr. Juniper's professional rooms
and surgery were at the back, close to the
side entrance.

The parlour was appropriated to the
young ladies, to their occupations and amusements. You never saw so untidy a place in
your life : one with the bump of order would,
upon entering it, have run away in dismay.
An old piano stood on one side, a key or
two missing and a dozen of its wires—it had
been the girls' practising piano when they
were children ; a set of book-shelves rose
opposite, piled with books in the greatest
confusion ; writing-desks lay about, some on
the floor, some tumbling off chairs ; sheets
of music, in all stages of tearing and copy-
ing ; work-boxes stood open, some without
lids, others without bottoms, their contents
all entangled together in one appalling mess :
pens, pencils, paints, French crayons, palettes,
chalks, work, thimbles, keys, notes, and

scrap-books were scattered everywhere;
whilst the chairs and the carpet were worn
and the table-covers frayed.

In this room, one evening in spring,
were all the girls, gathered round a blazing
fire, sitting, kneeling, or standing. The two
Miss Junipers were little, fair, slender young
women, very near-sighted, with hair remarkably light; whilst the daughters of the
late Mr. Battlebridge were tall, buxom girls,
with dark eyes and arched eyebrows; and
the youngest, Georgiana, half-sister to all the
others, was the beauty of the family. She
was now eighteen, and was thought a great
deal of by her sisters in general and by
herself in particular, and she had always
been indulged. They were bustling, accomplished, good-natured girls, much liked
in society: but their mother possessed
stricter notions of right and wrong than
does many a one who has been better born,

and she 'kept them under,' and saw more strictly after them than the girls liked. So they looked forward with ardent hope to the time when they should be married and become their own mistresses. Are there many girls who do not?—especially when they find they have left their teens behind them more years than they would care to tell.

On this evening, in their own parlour, they were chattering by firelight; just the nonsense that girls do chatter. Their theme was their father's new partner, who was expected on the morrow.

'I'll tell you what, Julia,' observed Miss Elizabeth Juniper, 'I have him in my mind's eye, exactly; just his portrait.'

'Let's have it, Bessy,' was the response of Miss Battlebridge.

'You remember that precious assistant papa had two years ago, with a nose like a

monkey's and a waist like an elephant's?
I wouldn't mind betting a new fan he will
be just such another man.'

'Green spectacles and all?'

'Green spectacles and all: or, perhaps,
an eye-glass by way of a change. We will
turn him over to Cicely; she used to admire the elephant; and he admired her, I
think.'

'You may call him an elephant and a
monkey now,' cried Miss Cicely Juniper,
nodding her head, 'but you were all setting
your caps at him then.'

'Just hark at Cicely!'

'He will not concern me,' interrupted
Georgiana, tossing back her pretty auburn
curls in the self-sufficiency of her youth and
beauty, 'for I know he will be as old as
papa. I shall begin to call him "uncle" as
soon as he comes.'

'Who's this?' exclaimed Kate Battlebridge, turning sharply round as the door opened, and a lady, attired in grass-green silk and white lace cap with pink ribbons, entered.

'It's only mamma. What are you coming in here for, mamma?'

'Why, the truth is, girls, I dozed off in the twilight, and the fire went almost out, so I am come in while they blow it up,' replied Mrs. Juniper. She was stout now and pretty red, and she *would* dress in bright colours; but her face was comely still, and her voice kindly as ever. 'Move away a bit, Bessy, and let one see the fire.'

Miss Elizabeth, pushing her sisters closer together, made room for Mrs. Juniper, without losing her own place in the circle.

'We have been wondering what the new doctor will be like, mamma.'

'Just like your silliness, girls: wondering your time away to waste. If I were you, I'd rather spend it putting this room straight. He'll be here to-morrow night, and then you'll see. I have been thinking what I had better get for his supper.'

'Tea, mamma,' interrupted the young ladies.

'Tea indeed!' ejaculated Mrs. Juniper indignantly. 'If any of you took a journey of six-and-twenty miles on a stage-coach, you'd be glad of something substantial at the end of it. What do you think of a fine savoury duck, nicely stuffed with sage and onions?'

The girls screamed, laughed, and did not approve of the dish at all. Bessy Juniper suggested an improvement.

'Have the tea nicely laid, mamma, with watercress and small rolls,' she said, 'and get in a little potted meat——'

'Potted donkey!' interrupted her

mother sharply. 'Do you think your papa is going to take a partner to starve him?'

'Potted meats are the fashion now,' Bessy ventured to remark.

'For full people; not for empty ones,' retorted the hospitably inclined lady. But before the discussion could be continued the door again opened, and a servant, looking in, said: 'Miss Erskine's here, young ladies.'

The five girls started up and hugged their visitor nearly to death. She was a very lovely girl, even for Worcester, with her dark-blue eyes, her exquisite complexion, and her raven hair: and though she was young, and slight, and gentle, she had a self-possessed manner and a haughty step.

'This is kind, Florence,' they cried; 'we have been so stupid all the evening! Take your things off. We were going to send for you to-morrow night, to see the lion arrive.'

'The what?' asked the young lady.

'Papa's new partner. He is coming by the Cheltenham coach. Bessy vows he'll be an elephant. And we are afraid he's old.'

'And, in the name of fortune, what difference should it make to you girls if he is old?' demanded Mrs. Juniper, turning round upon them, after shaking hands with Florence.

'Oh—he may not like our noise; our music, and that, if he is old,' answered Kate, glancing at the rest.

'The preliminaries are arranged, then?' remarked Miss Erskine.

'Yes, they are, my dear,' said Mrs. Juniper. 'So far as that the gentleman is coming for six months upon trial. A trial for both parties, you know, Miss Florence, which is only fair.'

'Of course it is,' said Florence. 'What is his name?'

'His name is the only item in the correspondence that we don't like,' said Mrs. Juniper. 'It's French. But he tells us he is thorough, genuine English. He is a Mr. de Courcy.'

'Formerly spelt Coursée, I believe,' said Julia Battlebridge. 'We are dying to see what he's like,' she continued in a low voice to Florence. 'And we have such pretty new dresses; challis, trimmed with green satin; we mean to put them on to-morrow night.'

'Put on what?' asked Mrs. Juniper, who caught the last words.

'Our best behaviour,' cried Julia, promptly.

But Mrs. Juniper's ears had been quick. 'Put on your new challis, will you! Look here, girls: you will not set up any of your nonsensical flirting with this gentleman. Neither your papa nor me would allow it: mind that.'

'Oh dear, *no*,' cried the girls promptly in answer. 'Why, we are expecting him to be as old as Adam! Mamma, don't you think your fire's burnt up?'

'Here's the Cheltenham coach; the one he will come by to-morrow evening,' exclaimed Cicely, as a resounding horn was heard. 'He is from London, Florence; but he took Cheltenham on his road down, to see some friends.'

'How that guard's a-blowing!' ejaculated Mrs. Juniper.

'And the coach has slackened its speed as if it were going to stop.'

'It is stopping,' said Mrs. Juniper.

'And at our house too! and a gentleman——Oh mamma!' broke off Cicely in excitement, 'he is come to-night!'

'Who is come?' asked Mrs. Juniper.

'Why, *he*, Mr. de Courcy. It must be! Now he is paying the guard—and now they are getting down his luggage—and now he is knocking at the door. What *shall* we do in these old merino frocks? Is there time to dress?'

'Bother to dressing!' put in the startled Mrs. Juniper. 'What's to be done about supper? Nothing on earth in the house but some cold hashed mutton and a round of beef in pickle. Ring the bell for the cook: or one of you girls run and tell her to come to me: she must send out for——Never trust me,' broke off poor Mrs. Juniper, 'if your papa's not bringing him in here!'

It was quite true. Mr. Juniper, seeing that the dining-room fire looked cold and black, ushered him into the girls' parlour, where he knew there was always a blazing one. He had been so long used to its litter that he thought nothing of it, and it never occurred to him to ask what a stranger might think. The girls, in spite of their dismay, took in the visitor's appearance at a glance.

A tall, prepossessing man, some years under thirty, gentlemanly in manner, free and pleasant in speech, with a rather sallow complexion, dark eyes, handsome features, and a winning smile. They could not well have seen one less like an elephant, or a monkey in spectacles. He laughed at their apologies about 'the wrong room,' and the 'girls' parlour,' and was at home with them at once.

Louis de Courcy—'Lewis,' it had been always called, he told them, according to English pronunciation—was born in England of French parents; his ancestors had been scared from their own land at the time of the great French revolution, and had never returned to it. Louis, the youngest of a large family, had grown up in the habits of an Englishman, and, but for his name, none could have suspected that any other country than this could put in a claim to him. He had been highly educated, was clever in his profession, and had fair prospects as regarded money. When he reached Cheltenham, he had found his friends there in deep distress on account of a death in their house, so he had come on to Worcester.

Before Mr. de Courcy had been a week in the surgeon's house he was a favourite with all its inmates, from Mr. Juniper himself down to Dick, the surgery-boy. Extremely clever, extremely eloquent, or, if we may be permitted to use the expression of Mrs. Juniper, 'favoured with the gift of the gab,' he took the good-will of people by storm, and the girls were convinced that a more desirable man as a husband-in-prospective was not to be found. But they could not all marry him: that was clear; so he was, by tacit consent, turned over to gladden the hopes of Georgiana, the others making themselves as agreeable with him as so many elder sisters. To Georgiana was left all the rights of flirting, and she did not fail to exercise them on her own account; de Courcy himself proving nothing loth, for he was fully awake to the charms of a pretty girl.

'It would be delightful for Georgy to be settled near us: and de Courcy would have to live quite close, being papa's partner,' the girls remarked one to another. 'We might spend half our time there.'

Indeed, to have a married sister thus established they had long regarded as the most fortunate thing that could happen to them—always excepting their own marriage

—for at her house they could flirt away at
leisure, secure from the discerning eyes of
Mrs. Juniper. So the girls set themselves
honestly to work to further the flirtation between de Courcy and Georgiana. In all
their walks and rambles Georgy was left to
his care : in all the evening parties, and they
went to many, he was sure to be her especial
cavalier : it was to her his arm was given,
when it was given at all : it was to her
singing his voice would be heard as second.
When he came into the girls' parlour for ten
minutes' chat, the seat next Georgy was at
once vacated to him : more than all, when
he would be in the humour to breathe words
of tender nonsense, in reality meaning nothing, but to a girl's heart implying much, it
was into Georgy's ear they were whispered.
De Courcy was by nature thoughtless, careless of consequences : he never reflected
that these attentions might appear to other

people to bear a serious meaning, or that he might be initiating Georgiana, for the first time in her life, into the art of love—to love *him*.

We must now turn to the subject and to the abode of Captain Erskine; who exemplified in his own person the truth of two of the attributes accorded to Worcester generally—poor and proud. Poor he was— very; and from no man living within the city's walls did exclusive notions of hauteur more fully shine forth than from Florence's father, Captain Erskine. In regard to family, he stood on the very loftiest pinnacle ; his ancestors had been the highest of the high. They were descended originally from royalty, and in later periods had owned lords and chancellors for cousins. He had his pedigree, setting forth all this, framed and glazed, and hanging up in his sitting-room. That he was of good descent appeared to be fact; but he boasted of it in so ridiculous a manner as to have acquired the name in the town, derisively applied, of Gentleman Erskine. He held up his head and literally looked down upon everyone. He was gracious with the Dean when he met him, and condescended to exchange bows with the prebends, but he looked straight over the hats of the minor canons ; of other people he took no notice. But fortune, alas, had not been so prodigal to Gentleman Erskine as his rank and his merits deserved ; therefore, he lived a most retired life. Want of means did not allow him to frequent the society of the great ; the little were beneath him. It was with much pinching and screwing that he contrived to make both ends meet, when the expenses of his pretty little cottage, just outside the town, containing his daughter and their one maid-servant, were settled at the end of each year. He had sold out of the army before his wife died, and what his small income really was no one knew.

Florence, brought up in these exclusive notions, had been allowed to cultivate the acquaintance of none. Whether the Captain expected a lord would drop from the sky some day and pick her up, he did not say, but he certainly allowed her no opportunity to mix with any of inferior rank, except the Junipers. Years back, when Mr. Juniper was attending the Captain professionally, he, the good-natured surgeon, pitying the isolated condition of the little girl, and the lack of means to afford her suitable instruction, proposed that she should come to his house daily, and partake (gratuitously) of the music and drawing lessons of Georgiana. Gentleman Erskine was too much impressed with the advantages of the proposal to decline it: though he considered the Juniper family amply repaid by the condescension. Hence had arisen Florence's intimacy at the surgeon's, and it was now so much a thing of habit, that it never occurred to her father to put a stop to it. Still he did not cease to remind Florence from time to time that though very worthy people in their way, those Junipers, they were persons whom she must not, even in thought, exalt to a level with their own sphere of life. Florence dutifully listened : but she wished with her whole heart that all such exclusiveness were buried at the bottom of the sea.

Shortly after the arrival of Mr. de Courcy, it happened that a distant relative of Captain Erskine's, a Mr. Stanton, was passing through Worcester, and halted there for a day. He was an old man, somewhat feeble, and in descending the stairs at the Hop-pole, then the principal inn of the city, he fell and broke his leg. He received also an internal injury; and, altogether, there was a doubt whether he would ever leave the town again. When able to be removed from the Hop-pole, apartments were taken for him in Foregate Street, and there he lay still, Captain Erskine dining and spending the evening of every day with him. It was said in the town that the Captain had expectations from him, and that of course it caused him to be attentive. Through these repeated absences from home of her father, Florence was enabled, unquestioned, to spend every evening, if she so willed it, at Mrs. Juniper's.

Oh, silly girls! you four elder Miss Junipers! You have but little forethought. You have set your mind upon Georgiana's gaining de Courcy, yet you daily throw into his society one more beautiful and not less attractive than she is! Florence was for ever being sent for by them: and she went. The evenings were growing long then, and sometimes all the girls in a body would take her home, and sometimes de Courcy himself was her only companion. Florence had never been brought into contact with a man so fascinating. It is true his manners to her were not of that free, gallant, openly-attentive nature displayed to Georgiana, but there was a subdued tenderness in them when alone with her infinitely more dangerous. Ah, readers! it is the old tale: Gentleman Erskine might impress upon his daughter the superiority of her descent to those around her, might descant upon it from night to morn; but he could not arrest this new, all-absorbing passion that was taking root in her heart. There is one thing makes its way in spite of all things—love.

It is dangerous to a girl's peace, let me tell you, aye, and to a woman's also, to be alone with an attractive companion of the other sex in the quiet evening hours. Florence would leave the surgeon's pretty early, by half-past eight or so, de Courcy with her to see her safely home. The house was not far off. When there, she would lay her bonnet and scarf on the table of the little drawing-room, and leaning out at the open window play with the jessamine and honeysuckle that grew round its frame ; not that she cared for jessamine or honeysuckle just then. De Courcy, sitting by her, would converse upon no end of subjects—I hardly know what, but if you have ever made one in these stolen interviews, you can tell. He was trying to improve her French accent ; teaching her to speak whole sentences in the language ; making her conjugate its verbs, *aimer* amongst the rest. Florence would begin her lesson : she was not very perfect in the verbs, especially the reflective verbs ;

they puzzled her : ' Je m'aime, tu t'aimes, il s'aime ; nous nous ———,' and there she would stop. ' Nous nous aimons,' de Courcy would break in, with his low, silvery voice. It really was a musical voice, but had it been of a crow's harshness, it would still have been silvery to her ear.

' Nous nous aimons,' de Courcy would go on, Florence repeating it after him, her heart beating, and her cheek blushing. He could see the blushes in the soft twilight of the evening, and she would turn her face from him, in its sweet consciousness, leaving nothing visible to his sight save its exquisite profile. They would rarely get to the end of the verb. De Courcy would begin upon some subject more attractive : the bright stars, perhaps, that were beginning to shine, or the pleasant look of the landscape as it cast forth its light and shade in the moonlight. The cottage stood upon a gentle eminence, and commanded an extensive view of the lovely county, than which none more beautiful can be seen in England. The long chain of the Malvern Hills bounded the landscape in the distance, and de Courcy was wont to declare that the clustering white houses beneath the hills of Great Malvern looked like fairy sea shells embedded amidst moss. The remark has been previously recorded elsewhere : but in truth it was often made. Thus they would wander on insensibly to dearer subjects, he reciting sweet verses at intervals, until they were both rapt in a maze of poetry and impassioned feeling. Byron's poems, Moore's strains, both more new to the world then than they are now; any romance, in short, that he could call to memory. And, during all this time, through the French, and the verbs, and the talking, and the poetry, he was sure to have stolen one of her hands, and to hold it clasped in his. Who would give five shillings now for the chance of Georgy Juniper?

One evening, either the young surgeon had remained too long, or Captain Erskine came home before his usual hour, but as they stood there, Florence was startled at the sight of her father coming up the road. She closed the window, rang the bell in hasty trepidation for candles, and just as the maid — who had had sweethearts herself, and was awake to things—scuffled them on to the table, and de Courcy rose and stood with his hat in his hand, Captain Erskine entered. A ceremonious bow between the two gentlemen, courteous on de Courcy's part, stiff and forced on the Captain's, and the former said good-night, and was gone.

'Why, bless my soul, Florence!' uttered the astounded aristocrat, looking round to be sure that he was not dreaming, 'it was that French fellow of Juniper's!'

She made some answer, quite unconscious what it was. Fortunately the Captain was too much ruffled to listen.

'Pray what brought *him* here?'

'I—he——' Florence began in her terror and agitation, and then she could get no further: as we all know, conscience does make the very best of us cowards. So she coughed a sharp succession of coughs, as if something had got into her throat, and turned to the window and began pulling about the muslin curtains: anything to gain time and calmness.

'What's the matter with the curtains?' he continued, sharply. 'I ask you what on earth brought that partner of Juniper's here? He was actually sitting down when I first saw him. Sitting down! my eyes could not have deceived me.'

'He brought this French book of Elizabeth Juniper's,' she stammered, indicating a
small French story-book ; and, so far, that
was true. Bessy had lent it to her and he
carried it home in his hand. 'And I was at
fault in my verbs, papa, and he offered to
set me right!'

True again. At least, tolerably so. Ah,
good sir, good Paterfamilias, groaning over
these pages and Florence's degeneracy, do
you imagine your owng irls tell you the
whole truth always? You were young and
in love once : how much did you tell in that
golden time?

'The devil take the French and their
verbs and all connected with them!' shrieked
Captain Erskine. 'How dare you stoop to
put yourself upon a level with a common
fellow of a doctor?'

'Dear papa,' said Florence, bursting into

agitated tears, 'I thought it no harm to ask him about the French verbs.'

'There's every harm,' retorted Gentleman Erskine. 'Do you forget, Florence, whom and what we are descended from? There's not a family in the county can boast the antiquity of ours; and here I come home and find a professional man's assistant sitting in the same room with you—*sitting*! —quite familiar—admitted to an equality! Some unheard-of French jackanapes, who may never have had a grandfather!'

'I am very sorry,' murmured Florence.

'Sorry! that's not the word for it: you ought to be ashamed. If the individual should come up again, let the servant take his message from him at the door, and dismiss him civilly—very strange that the Miss Junipers cannot send a maid with their commissions!'

Florence sighed, and was wisely silent.

'You are getting too old now, Florence,
to continue your intimacy with these
Junipers,' proceeded Gentleman Erskine
loftily. 'They were certainly kind to you,
and all that, and when you were younger it
did not so much signify ; but it won't do
now. Don't go there again. Or, at any rate,
only very rarely ; and let the acquaintance-
ship gradually drop.'

Captain Erskine stopped at that. He
supposed he had said all that was necessary,
for it never occurred to his exclusive mind
to suspect that his daughter could be more
tolerant on the subject of ' family ' than himself. What if he had been in a corner of the
room that very evening, and seen all the
tacit love-making? He might have vanished
through the floor with the shock, after the
manner of the imps in the pantomimes.

Thus Georgiana Juniper regarded Louis
de Courcy as her own particular knight, but

so did Florence Erskine. Each believed
that she possessed his heart, his sole alle-
giance. Each of them loved him in return.
Georgiana in only a light degree ; Florence
passionately and enduringly. Her intellect
was of a higher order than Georgiana's ; she
had more imagination, more dreamy sentiment: and it is precisely in such natures
that love takes the deepest hold.

And what thought Mr. de Courcy? It
was impossible that he could remain wholly
blind to the present aspect of affairs, and he
began to doubt whether he had not got
himself into what the Americans call a 'fix.'
That it was his own fault, entirely the result
of his own thoughtlessness, was no consola-
tion at all; quite the contrary. He could
not fail to see that Georgiana liked him, if
she did not love, and he awoke to the fact
that he was expected by the other girls to
make love to her. He had no true love to

give her ; all his hopes were concentrated on
Florence. The course of true love never yet
ran smooth ; we learnt that in our copy-
books : in this case there seemed to be a
ikelihood of its running rather rough. Why
could not Mr. de Courcy have fallen outright
in love with Georgy Juniper, and married
her with her parents' consent, as he might
have done, and so have found his future path
all straight before him ? Why should he
have remained wholly insensible (always
excepting the flirting) to her attractions, and
plunged over head and ears in love with one,
whom there was little more chance of his
winning and wearing, than there was of his
winning the stately daughter of the good old
bishop at the palace ? It must have been
fate, I think ; or, something in the air.

It has been asserted that love cannot
exist without jealousy. Love is wonderfully
sharp-sighted ; and, almost before there was

real cause, Florence and Georgiana became
jealous of one another. The elder girls were
not so soon awake to danger: but a word or
two, dropped by Georgy one day, in a pet,
opened their eyes.

They took alarm at once, lest the desirable match they had so pleasantly carved
out should drop through ; and Florence was
invited there no more. Not an hour did
de Courcy henceforth find for himself:
walks this evening, projected walks to-morrow evening, tea and parties always: and
he could not escape this, unless he had
been guilty of absolute discourtesy. Besides, he who had been so thoughtlessly
officious in seeking the society of Georgiana,
could not abruptly forswear it in rudeness
now.

Elizabeth Juniper resolved to put the
matter at rest: so the next time she was
alone with Mr. de Courcy she mentioned,

apparently quite incidentally, that Florence Erskine was engaged to be married.

'To be married!' uttered de Courcy, the red colour flushing into his sallow cheek.

'Did you not know it?' asked Elizabeth. 'She is to marry her cousin, Bob Erskine.'

De Courcy reflected. He was nearly sure he had heard Florence speak of a cousin 'Bob.'

'You don't know Gentleman Erskine,' she went on. 'His uncles and aunts, his godfathers and godmothers were princes and princesses, or something as grand, and he considers nobody upon earth good enough to associate with himself and Florence. Only to see him loom through the streets in winter, in that old worn fur-cloak of his with the scarlet lining, you would think all Worcester belonged to him! The little boys have to turn out into the gutter, for there's not room enough to pass him. Fancy such a man permitting his daughter the hazard of being addressed by any chance provincial! Not he, you may be sure. So he has secured for her one of the family, Bob Erskine.'

'Is this true, Bessy?' asked the young man.

'True as Gospel.'

'It is strange I never heard Florence allude to it.'

'It would be stranger if you had. Young ladies are not in the habit of telling of their matrimonial engagements. I may be engaged for all you have heard me say: so may Kate; or Georgy either.'

'Very true,' murmured de Courcy, with more abstraction than Bessy liked to see him exhibit at her latest allusion. 'Who is Bob Erskine? Where does he live?'

'Bob's a cousin, I tell you; the head of the Erskine family. He is in the Guards, or the Rifles, or some one of those crack regiments.'

'Can it be really so, Bessy?' he continued, still harping upon the theme. 'How did you come to know it?'

'From Florence herself. The last time Bob was staying with them, we girls charged her with its being so, and she admitted it. Though perhaps I ought not to have told you—it slipped from me unawares. It must be quite *entre nous*, mind you, Mr. de Courcy.'

'Certainly,' nodded the gentleman, unconsciously biting the top of his silver pencil-case into all sorts of forms.

'They are not to be married yet,' concluded Bessy. 'Captain Erskine considers Florence too young ; and Bob—well, Bob's young too.'

De Courcy took it all in—like an amiable sea-gull. Open and truth-telling himself, it

never occurred to him to suspect people of
being otherwise; certainly not a young lady
like Elizabeth Juniper. But though Bessy
had exaggerated a little, she had grounds for
what she said. They had teased Florence
about Bob Erskine when he was there, had
accused her of being engaged to him; and
Florence, after the custom of vain girls, had
laughed and simpered, but had not positively
denied it.

De Courcy felt miserable, for he had
become deeply attached to Florence Erskine,
and there grew up a sore feeling in his heart
towards her, that she should have fooled him
nearly on to telling her so.

Mr. and Mrs. Juniper were totally igno-
rant of all this flirting and scheming. Had
a suspicion of it entered their minds, they
would have given the girls a sharp trimming
all round.

After this, the young doctor did not go

near Florence, and if he heard of her being at Mrs. Juniper's, he kept out of the way. Thus he fell easily into the schemes of the Juniper girls, and flirted with Georgy as much as ever. ' Pour faire passer le temps,' he said to himself, ' rien d'autre.' He often *thought* in French.

One evening, Florence Erskine stood at that open window of her sitting-room; she had thus stood for many, many evenings, watching for one who did not come. Talk about de Courcy's feelings being sore—what were they to hers? Anger, despair, jealousy, and love by turns held possession of her. Oh that she should have suffered herself thus to become attached to a stranger—to a man despised of her father—to one who had sought her love only to fling it away in neglect!

Would he ever come again? Would those sweet hours, whose very remembrance seemed to renew life and love, ever return? Where was he? What had she done that he should thus desert her? As these thoughts dwelt in her mind, flushing her cheek, chilling her hands, agitating her whole frame, a noise, as of carriage-wheels, was heard, and Florence looked up. The road passed close by the side of the cottage, and the large, handsome four-wheeled chaise of Mr. Juniper came in sight, the surgeon driving, his wife beside him, and Julia and Kate in the back seat. Following, was the surgeon's professional gig, containing de Courcy and Georgiana.

The party bowed and smiled and nodded at Florence, the good-humoured surgeon calling out something her ear did not catch. *He* raised his hat as he looked at her; and, in the space of a minute, all trace of them, save the dust, was gone.

She shut down the window; she leaned

her throbbing temples upon her hands ; she gave vent to all the fierce jealousy that was raging within her. Never, never, she told herself in her passion, should her thoughts revert to that man again, save with scorn. And yet, the next minute, she caught herself indulging in a fantastic hope that he might come, even that evening, when his drive was over.

But he did not come; and the next night passed, and the next, yet he did not come ; and a whole week dragged itself by, and still he did not come. Florence was as one in a fever, tossing about by night and by day, and finding no rest.

One evening she was passing the surgeon's house when Mr. Juniper met her and took her in. They were just going to tea, and the hearty, kindly girls said she must stop. The whole family were present, and de Courcy looked at her keenly. She refused their invitation, but it was of little use ; one ran away with her bonnet, another with her gloves, and she sat down.

'What news is stirring, Florence?' asked the surgeon.

'None, that I have heard,' she replied. 'Papa received a letter from my cousin Robert this morning. You remember him?'

'Quite well.'

'He has been exchanging into another regiment, and embarks immediately for India. When he comes home again he will probably be an old man, he says.'

'Has he a wife yet, dear?' asked Mrs. Juniper slyly, for she had had her ideas of Florence and her cousin.

'Bob got a wife!' laughed Florence. 'Oh, no. He is not likely to take a wife.'

'My dear, you speak rather confidently.'

'I think I may,' replied Florence. 'When Bob had to go to Spain last month, papa, in writing, warned him against the attractions of the ladies there, saying he should not like to see him bring home a Spanish wife. Bob answered him that he was the last man in the world to think of any encumbrance of the sort, Spanish or English.'

De Courcy looked up, a strange, eager expression on his features. But, just at that moment, Miss Bessy was so awkward as to tilt over the cup of tea she was handing to him, and he had to start up and dance, for it scalded his legs.

A servant was desired to attend Florence home that night, but there stood de Courcy in the hall, hat in hand. 'Papa wants *you*, Mr. de Courcy,' exclaimed Bessy; 'he called to you as he went into the surgery.' So the young man, with an impatient exclamation on his lips, sought his senior partner, and Florence left with the maid.

But scarcely had she entered her home when he followed her in; and he stood there before her, his chest heaving, and his words coming from him impetuously.

'What must you have thought of me, Florence, all this time?' he began. 'You must either have judged me to be mad, or the most dishonourable man breathing.'

She trembled in her surprise and agitation, and felt faint, and could not answer. She certainly had not deemed him mad.

He took her trembling hands in his, he looked earnestly into her changing face, and went on, eagerly:

'Misapprehension has come between us, my love; whether designedly or not I cannot say. I see it all now. I was led to believe you were engaged to be married to your cousin—this Bob you have been talking of to-night.'

She uttered an exclamation of astonish-

ment. 'Oh, no, no! There never was anything between us; we did not care for each
other in that way. Bob is too poor to
marry—that is, too extravagant.'

'Yet I, in my credulity, believed it. It
has been as a dagger in my heart night and
day. For I love you, Florence, with a deep
and holy love.'

He drew her closer to him—he whispered
words of the most endearing tenderness—
he pressed her sweet face to his. And
then they both thought—and said—that
nothing should ever part their hearts again;
that they would live together, and for each
other, until their years of life had run into
the sear and yellow leaf.

But how many others have fondly vowed
the same, only to find them hereafter words
of vanity and vexation of spirit!

II.

THE PREDICTION.

PRESENTLY we are going to pay a day's visit
to Malvern. Not to Malvern as it has been
of later years and now is, but as it was
nearly a lifetime ago. It was then a lovely
little spot ; romantic, secluded, and beautiful.
Not a shop to be seen in it except the cake-
shop by the steep, leading down towards the
abbey, and the library. No gay place was
it in those bygone days, no rendezvous for
travellers in smart clothes, eager for pleasure
and society ; the few visitors seeking it were
really invalids, requiring pure air and peace.
It was half soothing, half painful to sit on
these beautiful hills, somewhere about St.

Ann's Well, and watch the scanty stock of visitors toiling up one by one. Soothing to recline there, undisturbed, on the green moss soft as velvet, looking round at the immense extent of landscape, so calm and still, where the only noise to break the quiet would be a distant sheep-bell; painful to gaze at the pale faces of the invalids, supporting themselves up the hill by the aid of a stick, and to listen to their troubled breathing as they gained the Well-room, and held the goblet under the spring. I have sat there many a day as a child finding no occupation but this watching and sympathy: picturing to my curious mind the outward and inward histories of these sick strangers; wondering whence they came, whither they were next going, where they lodged in the village. On some bright day the monotonous scene would be varied. A picnic party from Worcester, all gaiety and laughter, and baskets of provisions, would crowd merrily up the hill, and choosing a level, convenient spot, encamp themselves and their baskets on it, preferring this free, gipsy mode of enjoying a repast to the confinement of an hotel. Sometimes the day would pass on in almost complete solitude, no parties and no invalids, and then there was nothing to do but sit on the grass and build castles in the air, or to find a fairy-tale book, and be wrapt in a child's Elysium.

Oh the retrospect of those early days, our life's morning! when it seems that there is no care or sorrow in the world, or that, if there is, it cannot come near us; when we dream not that existence, the mysterious future so eagerly longed for, can be otherwise than it looks to us in those day-visions, sunny as the charming landscape around, bright as the blue sky above! To recall life as it looked then, with its glorious hopes and expectations, and to dwell on the troubled waters that have come rushing on since, well-nigh overwhelming heart and exist-ence!——Let us hasten on.

Many a merry donkey-party you might then see, toiling up the hills or cantering about the village. We had ours. One of them I especially remember. Twelve or fourteen of us, careless boys and girls to-gether, had the donkeys hired for us, and mounting in the village, just by the Unicorn, cantered off for a ride towards the Link; the old, sober heads of the company bringing up the rear on foot at a sober pace. The turn-pike-gate was open, and through it we dashed. But out came the turnpike-man, tearing after us, shouting and screaming. We all reined in and stopped. What was the matter? Matter indeed! we had gone through with-out paying. It was certainly true; and what was quite as true, upon searching

our pockets, those who had any, there was
not a single halfpenny to be found in one of
them ; what little we had possessed earlier
in the day had been spent in ' Malvern
cakes.' In vain we represented to the man
that ' those behind ' were coming up with
pockets full of money, and *they* were the
paymasters. He preferred to be on the
safe side, was inexorable ; so he made
us all dismount, and took off the white
cloths from the donkeys. What cared we?
We remounted without them, and scampered
on down the Link, leaving our astonished
old relatives to redeem the pledges. *Old* we
thought them then ; we should not think so
now. Lodgings at Malvern were then within
the bounds of a cautious purse, and there
was many an unpretending cottage, pictu-
resque without, clean within, that would let
you its best sitting-room, and its bedrooms,
for less than a sovereign per week, and give

you pleasant looks and civil attendance besides. Go and try them now, these Malvern
lodgings. Not that any cottages are left for
the experiment: they are transformed into
glaring villas and pretentious mansions.

Few places have changed as Malvern has
changed. Many a year ago it became the
emporium of fashionable society, who flocked
to it to try the ' water cure.' Patients wrote
their experiences to laud the system; our
greatest novelist of that day put forth an
account of the marvellous blessings it had
wrought on *him*, telling the world it had
made him young again. But the romance of
the place has gone for ever, and the peace of
seclusion it cannot know again.

The day's visit to Malvern was led by
Mrs. Juniper. Summer had come in. Mr.
de Courcy and Florence Erskine were
cherishing their secret love; while the
Juniper girls, perceiving it, made up their

minds to accept the inevitable, if it must be, and ceased to fight actively against it. They were good, right-minded girls, after all.

'I don't know whether I should altogether care to have him for my husband, though he is very nice to flirt with,' avowed Georgiana.

One hot afternoon the girls wrote a note inviting Florence to tea ; there was a secret they very much wished to impart to her.   On the evening previous to this, de Courcy had paid a short visit to Captain Erskine's house. And now, as Florence read the note, his impassioned words were still vibrating in her ears.

Of course she went : she would have gone to the end of the earth for the prospect of meeting *him*.   And it was when all were seated at the tea-table that Mrs. Juniper began talking of Malvern.

'Children,' she said, 'guess what I have been thinking of.'

'How should we know, mamma?' asked the young ladies.

'Why that we are perlite people, all of us, to have had Mr. de Courcy so long in our house, and never to have taken him to Malvern.'

'We can take him now,' said Bessy.

'To be sure,' heartily assented her mother. 'And you have a great treat in store, as you've never seen it,' she added to de Courcy. 'How we came to neglect it, I can't make out. Why, the first attention we think of paying to a stranger-friend—anyone from London, perhaps, or from far away on t'other side somewhere—is to take him to Malvern.' Mrs. Juniper's geographical knowledge was rather confused, especially as regarded the map of England and Wales.

'Let us make up a picnic,' exclaimed

Georgiana. 'And take our provisions, and dine on the hill.'

'With all my heart,' said Mrs. Juniper. 'You must come with us, Miss Florence.'

She looked up eagerly, and caught de Courcy's glance. Oh the rapture of a whole day spent on the Malvern Hills with him!

'When shall it be?' cried Julia Battle-bridge. 'When would it suit papa? To-morrow, papa?'

'If you like, child. Ask your mamma.'

'To-morrow!' echoed Mrs. Juniper, re-provingly; 'hadn't you better start to-night? You children have about as much brains as thought—and your papa no more either, in some things. Who is to get up a picnic at an hour's notice? There's the company to be invited, and got together, and there's the eatables. We shall want cold fowls, and tongue, and alimode beef; and some of you perhaps will be calling out for fruit tartlets. How can you have all this if you don't give time to cook and prepare it?'

Mrs. Juniper's remonstrance was unanswerable; so one of the girls dismally proposed the day after.

'That's as bad,' corrected Mrs. Juniper. 'Nobody goes picnicking on a Saturday.'

Finally, Monday was fixed upon. But Florence was wondering whether she could gain her father's consent.

Just at this period, Worcester was indulging surprise at a matter which was not in the common run of events. Some two or three weeks before a stranger had alighted in the town, had taken a lodging, and had caused it to be circulated in privacy and secrecy that he told fortunes. The surprise arose not from the simple action of his setting up as a fortune-teller, for that was not extraordinary, but in the fact that sundry predictions, spoken by this man to different people, were fulfilled in, to say the least of it, an unaccountable manner. Several of his visitors declared, with their eyes dilating and their hair standing on end near the organ of marvel, that he had told them things which no one ever knew, or ever could know, save themselves and Heaven. A few credulous people went to him at first; what they said sent others, and the man's fame grew. He was called the Wizard, and was never known in Worcester by any other name. It is no fictitious story that I am relating, though few people can be left now in Worcester who remember it. The better classes went to him in secret and would not have confessed to it for the world; some of them went in disguise. The man and his curious power had become an engrossing theme in the town; Mr. Juniper laughingly talked of it, and Mr. Juniper's daughters were wild to test it.

It was this which the girls wanted to confide to Florence; that they had made up their minds, after some qualms of conscience, to consult the Wizard.

Tea over, two of them drew her into their own parlour; Cicely and Kate; and they asked her if she would not like to accompany them.

'Are you all going?' inquired Florence.

'Not at once; the number might betray us, for where's there such a family of grown-up girls as ours?' replied Cicely. 'I and Georgy think of going first, and the other three some later night. Won't you come with us?'

'Not I,' laughed Florence, 'I have no faith. Wizards are clever men, I suppose; this one especially must be; but——'

'It will be such fun,' urged Cicely.

'We are dying to go. They say the most extraordinary things of him.'

'What if you get found out? If your papa hears of it?'

'How can he hear?' broke in Kate. 'We shall take every precaution; wear our shabbiest cotton frocks and garden shawls. The maids are going to lend us muslin caps to put on under our old cottage bonnets, so that we may pass for servant-girls. Why, if papa—or mamma, and she's sharper— were to meet us in the street they could not recognise us.'

'I know it will be great fun; and if I thought it would not be found out——' mused Florence. 'When do you go, Cicely?'

'We have fixed on Saturday night; the common people are then occupied, and there will be less chance of our meeting anyone at the Wizard's. Mamma won't miss us; we shall soon be there and back; and the others have promised to stay with her all the time. If she asks anything, they are going to say we are upstairs, brushing each other's hair. Do come, Florence.'

'I don't believe in it,' returned the young lady, waveringly.

'Why, they say he will describe one's future husband,' exclaimed Cicely, 'and so accurately, that if you were not to meet with him for years to come, you could not fail instantly to recognise him.'

A quick, burning colour dyed the face of Florence Erskine. If the wise man could indeed do this, she should know whether she was destined for de Courcy, and her doubts and fears would be set at rest.. And yet, the next moment, she laughed at the absurdity of her thoughts. 'Perhaps I will go,' she said to Cicely.

'Come in to tea on Saturday evening, and

we will steal away afterwards. You will not have a better opportunity. And remember, Florence, it is no such weighty matter after all, and if it does no good—if we don't hear anything worthy of belief, I mean—it can do no harm.'

'I will go with you; but mind, I have no superstition about me,' exclaimed Florence, looking suddenly up. 'I never had faith in these things, and never shall have. If I had faith, or any superstition, I should stay away.'

Cicely laughed. 'That is what every-one says.'

'For when I was a child,' proceeded Florence, speaking as if she were in a reverie, 'a woman who pretended to the gift of reading the future, as this man now pretends, foretold that if ever I should have my "fate cast," I should be at the end of my life.'

Kate gave a subdued scream. 'Then for the love of heaven stay away from him!' she exclaimed.

'Don't be silly, Kate,' said Florence, lightly. 'Do you believe that such power, pertaining only to the Most High, can be given to mortal man?'

Kate considered. Cicely shook her head. 'It may be given for a purpose at times,' Cicely said gravely. 'We cannot know. Either all these "Wise Men" are impostors, or none are; understand, I am speaking only of these wonderful soothsayers who are heard of perhaps only once in a century. If this strange man, astrologer, or whatever he may call himself, who has set himself down in Worcester, no one knowing "whence he cometh, or whither he goeth," like the wind—if it is given to him to discern and foretell the future, it may have been also given to her, who prophesied, you say, of your fate when you were a child. Do not go, Florence.'

'And we are living in enlightened times, and you think it necessary to give me this advice gravely?' exclaimed Florence, her lip curling with scorn. 'Oh, Cicely!'

'But if you are so mockingly incredulous, why go at all?' persisted Cicely. 'You will not believe anything he may tell you.'

'Surely you do not suppose I go to have *my* fortune told?' retorted Miss Erskine. 'Nonsense, Cicely! If I go at all, it will be for the fun of the thing; and to hear how far your credulity will allow him to dupe you and Georgiana.'

Cicely looked at her. 'I don't think you are quite so sceptical as you wish to make out, Florence.'

'Indeed I am.'

On the following day, Friday, Florence proffered the request to her father—that she

might be allowed to accompany the party to
Malvern.   It is eight miles from Worcester
by road.   Captain Erskine chanced to be in
a good humour with himself and everyone
about him, for Mr. Stanton had distinctly
intimated to him that he was substantially
remembered in his will, and the Captain
foresaw an end to his poverty.   So he
hesitated in his reply; had it not been for
his exuberance of spirits he would have
denied her at once.

'Who is going?' he inquired.

'Mrs. Juniper and the young ladies,'
replied Florence, not daring to intimate that
any strangers were to be invited.   'Mr.
Juniper will ride over in the afternoon if he
has time.'

'Juniper's carriage will not hold them
all,' cried Gentleman Erskine.   'And who's
to drive it?'

'The groom will drive, I suppose; and

they are going to have a post-carriage from the Crown,' answered Florence. 'It is two years since I went to Malvern, papa.'

'But going with these Junipers, Florence! I don't like that.'

'I do not know any one else to go with,' she timidly observed.

'Well, Florence,' he reluctantly conceded, 'for this once you may join them. But I do insist upon it that afterwards you set yourself resolutely to break up by degrees this intimacy. The girls may be pleasant and sociable, and all that, but they are beneath you. I am going out myself for a few hours on Monday,' he concluded, pompously.

Gentleman Erskine was going fishing. It was an amusement he delighted in. Sometimes he would be seen with his rod and basket, bearing off towards the Wear, at Powick; sometimes in the direction of

Bransford; sometimes in a totally opposite route. And there, arrived at the stream, he would sit with exemplary patience for hours in breathless silence, staring at the float, his line in the water, a worm at one end and a —what is it?—at the other, waiting for the fish to bite; his brain filled all the time with the greatness of the grandeur of all the Erskines.

It was growing towards sunset on Saturday evening when three figures, attired in cotton dresses, faded shawls, and plain straw bonnets with huge muslin borders underneath them, in short, looking like decent servant-girls, stole out of Surgeon Juniper's house, and walked quickly along the street, turning their heads from the gaze of the passers-by. The young ladies would fain have waited for twilight, but had not dared to make it so late. Fortune seemed to have

120 THE SURGEON'S DAUGHTERS

favoured them, for an old friend of Mrs.
Juniper's had dropped in to spend the
evening with her, and she never gave a
thought to what the girls might be about;
whilst Mr. Juniper and de Courcy were gone
to some famous medical lecture that was
being given that evening in the town.

They bent their steps in the direction of
Lowesmoor, in an obscure part of which
neighbourhood sojourned the Wizard.

'There's the house,' exclaimed Cicely in
a whisper, pointing to one of four low ones
in a row, with green shutters and narrow
doorways. 'I and Julia were walking by it
with papa last Sunday, and he laughingly
showed it to us; little thinking we should
ever make use of his information.'

As Cicely spoke, they halted before the
door, hesitating and deliberating, half fearful, now it was so near, of going on with the
adventure.

'You knock, Georgy,' continued Cicely.

' Knock yourself,' retorted Georgy. 'You have the use of your hands.'

'Shall we go back?' asked Florence, some impulse prompting her.

'Why, if we go back,' argued Cicely, 'they will laugh at us so dreadfully. Unless we say he had such a lot of people with him he could not see us. Are you afraid?'

'I afraid,' retorted Florence disdainfully. ' But we had better do one thing or the other, for we may attract attention standing here.'

' Oh, courage, courage,' exclaimed Georgiana, giving a smart rap at the door : ' don't let us have to say we took all this trouble about the caps and things for nothing.' And, before they had time to draw back, which perhaps they would have done after all, a boy opened the door and showed them into the presence of the Wizard.

He looked as little like a wizard, that is,

their ideas of one, as he could well look.
A thin old gentleman of sixty, dressed in
black with a white cravat, leaning back
comfortably in an arm-chair: they might
have taken him for one of the minor canons
sitting at his ease after dinner. The room
had nothing in it but chairs, tables, a carpet,
the usual ordinary furniture: of all apparatus
generally supposed to belong to the exercise
of the black art, the place was void.

'Is it the wrong house?' whispered
Georgiana to her sister.

'No, it is the right house,' said the
master, answering her thoughts, for her
words, they truly believed, he could not
have heard. 'Which of you shall I speak
with first? Let the others take a seat.'

He motioned towards a row of chairs
that stood against the wall at the end of the
room. The girls did not take the hint; all
three of them clustered round the table,

on which stood a curiously-constructed lamp, not known in those days, but common enough now. It gave a great light, and Georgiana, shrinking from its glare, pushed, almost imperceptibly, her sister towards the soothsayer. He resumed his seat, and looked at them, one by one.

'Why did you come to me in disguise?' he asked: 'with me it avails not. Take off those clumsy gloves,' he continued to Cicely; 'you have adopted them that your lady-hands may be hidden from me: but, until I have examined those hands, I cannot answer you a single question, or tell aught that you seek to know.'

She removed the old beaver gloves obediently, almost reverently, as if she were in the presence of a master-spirit—perhaps she thought she *was* so. Before looking at her hands, he took out of a drawer a pack of cards, giving them to her to shuffle and cut, and he then placed them, one by one, their faces upwards, upon the table. They were singular looking; not playing cards at all; each card presented a different and intricate picture, and was inscribed with curious Egyptian names.

Cicely waited, her hands stretched out to display their palms. Now the wizard would carefully examine the hands, a microscope to his eye; now, without the microscope, he would study the cards on the table. Presently he laid the glass down, and looked in Cicely's face. The other two stood in silence, amusement displayed on the countenance of Florence Erskine.

'You need not have troubled yourself to come here,' he began abruptly, addressing Cicely, 'for I can tell you little more than you already know.'

'What do you mean?' she stammered involuntarily; and he resumed.

'Your course will be marked with no event of sufficient moment to be set forth here: neither of joy nor sorrow. As a ship sails calmly along a smooth sea, so will you pass peacefully down the stream of your maiden life, until its race shall be run.'

'But who will be my husband?' inquired the eager Cicely.

'You will never marry,' he returned.

'Never marry!' echoed the girl.

'No. You had a chance once, and you threw it away. You will not have another.'

Georgiana stared in amazement at the joke of Cicely's having received an offer, and *rejected* it. But look at Cicely—at her glowing colour: that alone will tell you his words are true. The assistant-surgeon, designated by her sisters as the elephant, the monkey in spectacles, had made Cicely an offer in secret, and she had refused it.

'And be thankful that your life is destined to be so uneventful,' continued the speaker to her. 'There are two paths in this world; one is of peace—and a very small one it is, but little frequented; the other is full of thorns. To few people indeed is it given to tread the former; but you are one of them.'

The dismayed and angry Cicely felt her face growing hot and cold by turns, as she listened to this most unwelcome prediction; and she only awoke from her astonishment to hear the man addressing her sister. Georgiana had removed her gloves at his desire, touched the cards as Cicely did, and waited. Florence had drawn nearer, and she saw, what she had never noticed before, that the inside of Georgiana's hands, even to the ends of the fingers, were completely covered with lines; small lines, crossed, and re-crossed again. The old man sat looking at them with his glass to his eye.

'Your fate in life will be widely different from your sister's,' he said at length, 'for you will meet with, and endure, more cares than I should choose to tell you of.'

'And not be married either, perhaps!' burst forth the indignant Cicely.

'You will be married in God's own good time,' he continued to Georgiana, taking no heed of Cicely. 'And though your life will be full of cares, as I now predict, there is no cause for you to be dismayed, for it will not be without its compensations. Your home will lie in a foreign land, one washed by the troubled waters of the Pacific Ocean. *He* is there now; and you will not see him yet: not for years to come.'

'Not there *now?*' exclaimed Georgiana, surprised out of the remark.

'May be your thoughts are running upon one nearer and dearer,' he rejoined: 'but neither of you'—and he looked alternately at Georgiana and Florence—' will marry *him*; so let there be no more bitter feeling between you. You have wasted by far too much on these dreams already; dreams that for both of you will come to nought. The wife destined for *him* is as yet a child, sporting in her mother's home : neither of you will ever be more to him than you are now.'

Georgiana, in her surprise, could not find ready words of answer. Florence was indignant.

'You are mistaking your vocation, sir,' she haughtily exclaimed. 'I did not come here to have my fortune told.'

'I will not tell it, young lady,' he quietly replied. 'Nevertheless, I should like to be allowed to take a closer look at your hands. Their marks strike me as being peculiar.'

Florence's hands were resting on the table; she had taken off the large, uncomfortable gloves assumed for disguise. Making no objection, she moved them nearer to him in scornful compliance ; perhaps in curiosity. The Wizard examined them long and attentively, glancing aside at the cards from time to time in silence.

'I did not come to you for advice or remark of any kind,' repeated Florence, when he looked up.

'So you have informed me : and I know that all I might say would be worse than despised. Yet, if you would listen to me, I could save you even now.'

'Save me from what?'

'Nay, why question me? Have you not warned me that you wish to hear nothing?'

'I wish to hear this,' she answered, her tone of scorn growing deeper. 'Tell it me, I beg of you.'

'It will make no difference whether I do or not,' remarked the man, as if speaking to

himself. 'From the fate which is threatening you: and which appears'—bending
again over her hands—'to be drawing very
near now——'

'Pray what is the fate?' she interrupted.

'I cannot say. I do not know.'

Florence laughed a derisive laugh. 'Oh,
thank you: that is quite sufficient. You
would warn me to avoid some fate or other,
but you don't know what! Thank you,
sir, once again, for your valuable advice. I
have already said I did not come to seek it.'
She made him a half-mocking curtsey, and
turned to her companions, saying that as
their business was over, it was time to be
going. The young ladies turned to leave,
and the Wizard rose.

'To you who did come to seek it, I have
no more to add,' he said. 'Your life,' looking at Cicely, 'will be one of uneventful

calm, bearing for you no great pleasures and no great pains. And yours,' turning to Georgiana, 'will be one scene of cares and crosses from the day you relinquish your father's name; and his for which you will exchange it, is to you as yet that of a stranger: but do not forget that the life will bring to you its compensations. There is nothing more; so go back quickly, all of you, whence you came.'

The two sisters laid, each, a heavy piece of silver on the table, as they turned to depart. Florence laid nothing. She was about to follow them, when the old man placed his hand upon her shoulder, his strange, deep-set eyes riveting their gaze on hers.

'You have good seed in your heart,' he said earnestly, 'and your faults are but those of youth and thoughtlessness. I will not have it on my conscience that I suffered you

to pass this threshold without a warning,
unavailing though it will be. For the next
three or four days, say until Monday—or—
perhaps—Tuesday—say until Tuesday shall
have glided into the womb of the past, keep
strictly the Commandments; break not one
either in the spirit or the letter: and then
years of happiness may yet be yours.'

'And if I do not?' asked Florence.

'I have told you that you will not. In
less than the time I have mentioned to you,
you will, I fear, have gone whither we are
all hastening.'

'If danger threatens me,' she persisted,
'why not tell me its nature, that I may
avoid it?'

'In asking the question, you are but
mocking still,' he sadly said, 'but I will
answer it. That some great danger threatens
to overtake you, is certain; its precise nature
I know not: such close knowledge is not

given us. But it seems to me that it will arise out of some fault of your own—I think, self-willed disobedience. Now go: I have fulfilled my duty.'

He resumed his chair as he spoke, and the three girls turned and were gone.

'Of all canting, story-telling impostors,' broke out Cicely, before they were well in the street, being unable longer to control her exasperation, 'that wicked old animal beats all.'

Cicely truly believed so. For he had said she would never be married: and if all the wise men breathing had sworn to that, she would not have given credence to it.

'You don't believe in him, then?' said Georgiana, whose spirits seemed rather subdued by the visit.

'Believe in him!' retorted Cicely. 'I would give a thousand pounds, if I had it, to be Mayor of Worcester for one day, just to have him put in the stocks. The wretched old idiot!'

Florence Erskine remained silent, her reflections full of uneasiness and perplexity. She had maintained during the visit a mood of contempt and disbelief : to say that she came away in it would be wrong. The extraordinary power with which that man, wizard or no wizard, divined her and Georgiana's most secret feelings, puzzled her : their jealousy of each other, which she had believed could be known to none; the positive assertion that neither of them would marry de Courcy ; with the solemn prediction that in a space of time which might be counted by hours, some untoward fate threatened to overtake her, *he* evidently pointed to death! Mixed with these thoughts came recurring the remembrance of that tale of her childhood—that should she ever have her fortune told, she would be

at the end of her life: this man had now
said she was at the end of it.

'I told you,' she laughed, but the laugh
sounded bitterly hollow in her companions'
ears—'I told you what you would meet
with, Cicely; you will believe in fortune-
tellers now! And he—he—that daring
charlatan, presumed to warn ME against
breaking the Commandments!'

Wrapping their shawls round them, and
drawing their bonnets over their faces, they
hastened through the now lighted streets,
and gained their home and entered undis-
covered.

Sunday was the next day. In the afternoon Captain Erskine went as usual to visit
his relative, and Florence afterwards took
her way to Mrs. Juniper's, the girls having
invited her. The disagreeable impression
left by the Wizard's words had faded away;
reason had reasserted its power, and

Florence was herself again. The surgeon's family usually attended church on Sunday evenings, but this night two or three of the girls had themselves excused on the score of the heat, and stayed at home to chatter. When Florence made ready to go home, a servant was waiting to see her thither; but de Courcy, coming in at the moment, told the maid her services were not required, and went with Florence himself.

They walked away towards her home, in the sultry, overpowering air, their pace so slow as to be scarcely perceptible, she listening to his honeyed words. Ah! she thought not now of the old Wizard and his predictions; when with *him*, the fulness of her happiness was all in all. And thus conversing with each other, they neared the cottage. No other dwellings were near to it, no prying eyes could be on view, and de Courcy drew Florence's arm within his, little conscious, either of them, that the worst eyes of all were looking on.

At the window of his small drawing-room stood Captain Erskine. He had come home betimes to make certain preparations connected with his fishing-tackle and bait for the morning's excursion. In the midst of which, happening to look towards the road, he saw his daughter sauntering up the hill, comfortably leaning on the arm of——

Of whom? The Captain applied his double eye-glass to his eye, wiped it, turned it, and tried it again. Why—good saints protect himself and his outraged ancestors ! —it *was* that connection of Juniper's ! They have reached the little gate now, and Florence's hand is held in his as he leads her through it ; and Gentleman Erskine's grizzled hair raises itself on end with horror, and his gaze glares on his insulted pedigree, hanging opposite, and he brings his indignant face into close contact with the window-panes.

Florence saw him ; and, turning sick with apprehension, wished de Courcy a hasty good-night and went in.

Captain Erskine was by no means a meek man, but never had Florence seen him give way to passion so violent. A half doubt of the truth flashed across his brain. Florence he knew was beautiful ; while this fellow, he half acknowledged to himself, was what women and fools might call attractive. But the doubt was dismissed at once : for Gentleman Erskine's exclusive mind could no more bring itself to suspect Florence capable of an attachment for a man in the position of de Courcy, than for the begrimed official who periodically went up his chimneys ; and indeed the ropes on which he himself stood were so exalted, that he could see little difference in the position of the two, the dispenser of medicines and the *ramoneur*. Oh, terrible disgrace!—she had walked with this man (as he supposed) through the open streets! Worcester had seen her leaning upon the arm of an apothecary, that obscure *émigré*, who had never known his grandfather! How could this stain be wiped out?

As a preliminary step, when his rage had somewhat expended itself, Captain Erskine forbade his daughter, in the most positive terms man could use, to join the party to Malvern on the morrow. She shivered, she cried, she pleaded for a retraction of his prohibition; all in vain. She might with as much effect have set on and petitioned Jupiter.

'What shall I say?' she sobbed. 'I told them you consented, and they expect me. What excuse can I offer now?'

' Excuse to them !' he cried indignantly ;
' the obligation is on the other side. Make
none. Or say it is my pleasure, if you
choose : but, go you do not.'

' Oh, papa ! '

' How dare you oppose your will to
mine, even in thought?' he demanded.
' Are you out of your mind? I forbid you
to think or to speak again about their scam-
pering Malvern party. I would rather lock
you up, Florence, than suffer you to join it.
Disobey me if you dare.'

When Florence rose the next morning,
her head aching and her eyes heavy, she
found a brief, stern note left for her by her
father, who had departed on his fishing excursion. It reiterated his prohibition of the
previous night ; once more enjoining her not
to disobey him. She wrote a line to Mrs.
Juniper, saying she was unable to accompany
them, and sent it. In answer to it came

Mr. de Courcy, requiring, in Mrs. Juniper's name, to know the why and the wherefore. Florence simply said her father wished her not to go; but of his positive prohibition and his violence she did not like to tell. De Courcy supposed Captain Erskine's objection might be put down to the score of the heat, which was excessive. He treated the prohibition lightly. Persuasion is wondrously effective when uttered by loved lips, and Florence wavered. She made a compromise with her conscience, and assuring *it* that no persuasion should induce her to disobey her father by going to Malvern, she yet consented to accompany de Courcy to Mrs. Juniper's, to tell them in person that she could not go.

It was then ten o'clock, the hour fixed for starting. The party of invited friends were assembling, all eager and joyous, the carriages waited at the door, and Florence was tempted on all sides: her scruples were assailed, her somewhat confused accounts of her father's 'wishes' laughed at.

'The heat!' exclaimed Mrs. Juniper, catching up de Courcy's notion. 'Well, it's bad enough to-day, child, goodness knows; but it won't melt you.'

Mrs. Juniper added some convincing arguments, their matter sensible enough, the girls said go she should and must, de Courcy whispered a passionate entreaty, while the good-natured surgeon declared he would bear all the blame and appease Captain Erskine. And Florence, overpowered by their persuasions and her own yearnings, at length yielded, her conscience pricking her, and her better judgment fighting a fierce battle.

It was half-past ten when they started, eighteen or twenty of them, a goodly cavalcade. Two post-carriages from the Crown in Broad Street, and the surgeon's chaise, de Courcy driving the latter.

'You will go with *me*, Florence,' he had said to her, as they all stood on the threshold of the door. But, even as he spoke, Georgiana Juniper mounted, without assistance, into the front seat of her father's carriage; and Mr. Juniper, coming up, took Florence's hand, and placed her in one of the large ones by the side of his wife.

The postboys started. Down Broad Street, over the bridge, increasing their speed as they bowled along the open road leading to St. John's, and lessening it as they came to the houses. St. John's passed, they drove through the turnpike-gate, and were fairly on the road to Malvern in all the heat. None could remember such heat as hung that day over the Faithful City.

Mrs. Juniper complained piteously.

'What's my face like?' she suddenly asked. 'Is it crimson?'

'I never saw any crimson so red, mamma,' answered Julia, turning round from the box, where she was seated with young Mr. Parker, who was reading for the Church, there being a living in his family. He had just come down from Oxford, after being plucked in his Little Go.

'What a mercy it is that we thought of bringing that bottled perry!' continued Mrs. Juniper. 'As to the ale and wine, I don't think we ought to touch it till the sun's gone down, unless we'd like to be laid up with brain fever. I never felt such a day as this.'

'Nor anyone else in this country, ma'am,' observed young Parker. 'It is said that strange old Wizard has predicted this day will be a memorable one. I think he is about right for once.'

Julia Battlebridge turned again and glanced at Florence with a meaning look. Florence sat silent and pale. She did not absolutely fear the words the strange man had said to her; she did not positively fear that old prediction of her childhood; and yet both kept floating in her brain, mingling with the thoughts of her own disobedience, and what would be the anger of her father. That strange injunction of the Wizard's, bidding her not break any of the Commandments, had come back to her with vivid vehemence. She had listened in resentment to the unnecessary warning, haughty pride buoying up her own self-sufficiency—she, Florence Erskine, break a Commandment! Yet, not thirty-six hours had elapsed before she had fallen into the snare and the sin: she had broken the one which says, 'Thou shalt honour thy father and thy mother.'

Wick was passed, and then the old and

most dangerous bridge at Powick, and, passing the turnpike-gate, the horses bore up
the ascent, turning off opposite the Lion.
Soon the windings of the road brought the
towering hills in view, with their various
hues, blue, brown, green, and golden; and
de Courcy saw that his pretty white sea-
shells were indeed houses. Away cantered
the postboys, on to Newland Common, its
geese as plentiful as ever, leaving on their
left the turning to Madresfield, Lord Beau-
champ's seat. The Swan, with its swinging
signboard, passed on the right, the horses
began their slow pace up the Link, noted for
its upsets, and the party reached the village
of Great Malvern at last.

They drove to the Crown, and alighted.
The carriages were to be left there. Mrs.
Juniper was shown to the pleasantest sitting-
room with the lovely view, ordered a plate
of sandwiches for those who wished to par-

take of any, and said the party would return for tea at six o'clock in the evening. It was a programme often carried out: luncheon on the hills; tea at the Crown or the Bellevue.

Meanwhile the hampers of provisions— Mrs. Juniper's fowls and tartlets and à-la-mode beef—were taken from the carriages, now surrounded by a shoal of donkeys, with their drivers—sunburnt women, boys, and girls.

'Are we to ride or walk up?'

'Who asked the question on such a day as this?' cried young Mr. Parker, looking down from the balcony. 'Mrs. Juniper shall have that one,' pointing to a large strong grey donkey. 'And, I say, my good donkey-women, give an eye to your saddles: they have a habit of turning, you know.'

Mr. de Courcy chose to walk: not a

very wise determination, as Mrs. Juniper
told him, with the thermometer at its present
height. *She* did not know that the heat
and the climb were to him as nothing,
whilst he could thus keep by the side of
Florence Erskine. And so they commenced
their ascent of the hill, towards St. Ann's
Well, and Mrs. Juniper sincerely wished
there was a carriage-way to it, that she might
avoid the zigzag path of the jolting donkey.
In later years one was made.

They took de Courcy to an elevated spot,
and then made him turn suddenly to look
at the glorious beauty of the scene. The
amazing expanse of prospect extending out
around; the peaceful plains, lying broad and
distinct; the blending together of wood and
dale ; the striking contrast of the green
fields with the golden hue of the ripening
corn ; Bredon Hill there, the Old Hills here,
hills everywhere; the few mansions scattered

about with a sparing hand, giving life to the landscape: and Worcester, fair to view, lying not far off, with its fine old cathedral and St. Andrew's tapering spire.

'Yes, it is very beautiful,' sighed de Courcy, drawing a deep breath of reverence as he lifted his hat. 'Great indeed are the glories of God's marvellous works!'

Mrs. Juniper's voice brought him back to common life. 'If you'll believe me, them silly apes are going on to the top!'

Turning from his somewhat prolonged reverie, de Courcy saw that the younger members of the party were continuing their way up the hill: the elder ones had dismissed their donkeys and were gathered in and about St. Ann's Well.

'Have you lost your wits, you young people?' screamed out Mrs. Juniper again.

'No, mamma,' replied Bessy, looking round. 'Why?'

'If you ride to the top in this heat you'll be half dead.'

'Oh, we don't care for that. We shall be back for dinner.'

Mrs. Juniper sat down inside the room at the Well. Some of the more active ones began to unpack the hampers. One gentleman, an old Worcester lawyer, who was rather puffy, threw himself flat on the grass, wishing he could find a breath of air. In vain : the atmosphere was still as death.

'Decidedly those young ones will be broiled,' he remarked.

'Why, here they are, back already!' exclaimed Mr. Parker's mother, as she caught sight of the white cloths of the donkeys, slowly winding round from the heights above. 'We shall see how they feel after their broiling.'

'I have heard tell of women in Ingee,' remarked Mrs. Juniper, extending her head

outside to get a view of the broiled, ' who
have voluntarily sat right down in a huge
fire to be roasted alive. I'd not say that
there can lie much choice between that and
going up the hill to-day, as them geese
were doing; especially if it was a-foot like
Mr. de Courcy.'

'It was impossible to endure it,' called
out Cicely in explanation. ' I believe, if we
had gone on, we should have felt ready to
drop, as mamma said, and the poor animals
too. So that's why we are back again.'

Heavy and listlessly passed the time, in
the unbearable heat, till they sat down to
dinner, and sincerely did they wish their excursion had been deferred to a more pro-
pitious day. But young and healthy people
cannot be still long; and some of them,
when dinner was over, began to wander up
the hill again. The heat was really terrible, not perhaps quite so burning as it had

been in the morning, for the blazing sun had
gone in, but the oppressive, sultry sensa-
tion had increased.   It seemed as if they
could scarcely draw breath; and ominous
clouds of copper colour were gathering in
the sky.   Unheeding the weather, and re-
gardless of fatigue, de Courcy and Florence,
side by side, at length reached the top of the
hill: their companions had dropped off one
by one, and they were alone.   There they
stood some time, that he might admire the
vale of Herefordshire ; a fine prospect also,
but not equal to the magnificent one on the
other side.   And then, turning to the left,
they continued their way on the hill's summit,
and gained the little round building, scarcely
larger or higher than a good-sized watch-
box, known as Lady Harcourt's Tower.

Here they entered and sat down ; and
de Courcy, drawing her to his side, whispered
once more his words of love.   Eloquent

words they were, more eloquent than they
need have been, for where love reigns in a
heart, as it did in hers, eloquence is needed
not; and she, lost in the perfect rapture of
the moment, put her compunctions of conscience aside.   She forgot her disobedience;
she forgot the certain refusal of her father
to sanction the future; she braved the
thought of his anger, and promised to be
the wife of Louis de Courcy.

A flash of lightning startled them ; and,
as they rushed outside the tower, a long,
loud, frightful echo told that the storm had
begun.   Never, perhaps, had a storm come
on with more rapid violence.   The clouds
had gathered together, black, lurid, angry,
the forked lightning playing amongst them ;
the thunder reverberated in the hollows of
the hills ; and the atmosphere appeared as if
tainted with death, it was so still and
terrible.

'We must make the best of our way down, Florence,' hastily cried de Courcy.

But there came, flying to the top of the hill, five or six of their party—the lawyer before mentioned and his daughter, two of the Juniper girls, and a lad of fifteen and his sister. They had been close to the summit when the thunder commenced its roaring, and were running to take shelter in Lady Harcourt's Tower.

'I do not like it,' interposed de Courcy, as they were about to enter. 'We shall be safer going down the hill than there.'

'Not at all,' dissented the lawyer, who was puffing with his recent exertion. 'I remember, when a boy, a party of us being overtaken in this very spot by a most violent thunderstorm. We shut ourselves in here —there was a door to the place then—and were quite safe and comfortable; whilst in the valley below there were two cows and a milkmaid killed.'

Still de Courcy did not like it; but not one was willing to descend the hill with him and brave the fury of the storm, preferring the shelter of Lady Harcourt's Tower. The situation was appalling enough. Perched on the summit of one of the highest of the Malvern hills, the valley beneath them appeared as if it were miles away, and they planted in the air, on that narrow ledge between the earth and the sky, amidst all the roar and battle of the elements.

The storm increased in violence; peal succeeded flash, and flash succeeded peal without an instant's cessation; the heavens were in a blaze of light from one extremity to the other, and a noise, as of a thousand cannons, seemed bursting close overhead. The poor girls were fearfully terrified. De Courcy tried to reassure them, but could not succeed : a scream from one, a shriek from another ; tears and sobs ; exclamations, that the lightning blinded and the thunder deafened them, were mixed with murmured prayers and dread whispers that they should never get down again alive. Florence was quiet, betraying less terror than the rest. Why was it ? Because she was by the side of *him*, her lover; and so all-absorbing to her was the consciousness of her love for him, that other emotions, and even the dread of danger, were partially lost in it : his protection seemed to be all-sufficient for security, as it was for happiness. De Courcy had thrown his arm round her and drawn her to his side, where she quietly stood, her face hidden against him, and her heart beating with its sense of bliss. Cicely Juniper he had drawn to him on the other side.

'There !' he exclaimed, pointing to a

distant part of the heavens. It was a small
ball of fire, darting down to the earth. The
sight was momentary: before the others
could look, it was gone.

'I must say I wish we were safe down,'
exclaimed the old lawyer. 'I wonder how
Mrs. Juniper and the rest feel at the Well?'

Before the words had well passed his
lips there came a vivid flash, a terrific peal,
and a scream from Cicely Juniper, who
declared the tower was shaking. It may
have been her fancy, or it may have been
that the tower did shake with a shock of
electricity, the others felt nothing; but
Florence Erskine had fallen on the ground
at de Courcy's side. There was no perceptible change in her countenance, except that
it was white and still.

'She has fainted!' exclaimed the lawyer,
stooping, and pulling at her hand.

'It is the faintness of DEATH!' shuddered

de Courcy, bending down his ashy face. 'I fear, I fear it is death.' He raised Florence in his arms as he spoke; he called her by every endearing name, unmindful now of the ears of those around; he pressed his white cheeks to hers, vainly hoping to feel signs of breath and life. But there was no further life for Florence Erskine in this world, for she had indeed been struck and killed by lightning. And when the wailing and terror-stricken party returned that night to Worcester, carrying the dreadful tidings with them to Captain Erskine, the ill-fated young lady, cold and dead, had to be left at Malvern.

It had, in truth, been a remarkable and fatal day, as the strange man, the Wizard, had foretold. On the following morning, Cicely, in her horror and perplexity, disclosed to Mr. Juniper the particulars of their visit to this man, with his prediction regarding Florence, and the surgeon went to Lowesmoor at once to seek him out. But he had disappeared; he was gone, none knew exactly when, certainly not whither; he had left the city.

Mr. Juniper plied the landlady of the house with questions. She said that on the Sunday evening he had called her to his presence, paid her what little claims she had against him, with something over, and told her he should probably leave on the morrow. On the Monday morning while he was at breakfast she went upstairs to make his bed, and there she saw his little black portmanteau ready packed. But she did not see him leave the house, or know at what hour he really went away.

Mr. Juniper could discover no more than that. Yet he would have liked to do so: he would have liked to put a few questions to the man, for he felt intensely puzzled by

him.   He had his reasons.   This Wizard, or
whatever he was or might call himself, had
betrayed a knowledge of things which it
seemed impossible (unless by more than
human inspiration) he could have known or
learnt in any way.   One instance shall be
given.

At a short distance from Worcester there
lived two small respectable farmers, related
to one another and occupying adjoining
farms.   On the Saturday morning, the same
day on which, later, the Juniper girls paid
their visit to the Wizard, a daughter of each
of these farmers walked into Worcester as
usual to keep market: their baskets of
cream-cheese, poultry, eggs, and butter being
conveyed thither by a man on horseback.
They wrangled as they walked : Phillis D.
had brought her little sister with her, which
displeased Esther J.   'It's not my fault,'
pleaded Phillis, defending herself warmly.

' When I came downstairs from putting my things on, there was Sally all ready in her bonnet and tippet, and mother said she was coming with me. How could I help bringing her, I'd like to know? I did try; I said the walk would be too much for her this hot weather; but mother answered me shortly that the child was looking puny, and it would do her good.'

' All the same, you should have somehow contrived not to bring her just to-day,' retorted Esther.

For these two young women were intending to get their fortunes told. Having heard the marvellous things said of the Wizard, they wished to benefit by his divinations as well as other people did, and perhaps get promised a husband apiece in some flourishing young farmer. The visit had been planned for the previous Saturday, but a matter prevented its being carried out;

so they meant to pay it to-day without fail : if it were put off yet for another week, the Wizard might have left Worcester. Of course Sally's presence was a tremendous drawback, but they must make the best of it.

By dint of selling their excellent wares cheaper than usual, they were at liberty before one o'clock and bent their steps from the market house down to Lowesmoor ; promising Sally dire punishment for all time to come if she ever breathed a word of what she was about to see and hear. But these warnings, administered in going through Silver Street, produced an effect which they had not calculated upon. The child was seized with intense terror. She had heard of the Wizard, and entertained a most un- reasoning fear of him, fully believing he would eat her up at sight, as the wolf ate up Red Riding Hood. Sally was a pretty little girl of ten years old, constitutionally timid, and she burst into sobs and cries. The young women shook her and slapped her. Finding that did little good they presently, after turning out of Silver Street, bought her some gingerbread nuts and bull's-eyes—which in a degree soothed the tears if not the fear.

The Wizard was alone when they entered. While he proceeded to tell the fortunes of the elder girls, the little one was placed on one of the chairs at the end of the room : but she wept aloud, and trembled from head to foot. Once it seemed to distract the Wizard : he paused in what he was saying, and looked around.

'Who is the child ? What is she crying for ?'

'She is my sister, sir, and she was afraid to come here,' answered Phillis D. 'Sally, you naughty girl, hush your sobs directly.

Who do you suppose is going to harm you ? '

' There is nothing here to harm you, my child,' spoke the wise man, gently.   ' Don't be afraid.'

This address seemed to have quite an opposite effect from the kindly one intended. Sally, after a moment's silence from dumb terror, went on sobbing more than ever.

At the close of the interview, when the young women were departing well satisfied, for they had each been promised fairly good luck in life as well as a husband, the Wizard rose and put his hand upon Sally's shoulder.

' Cry on, my child, for you have good cause to do so,' he said to her with sad impressiveness.   ' You will reach home to find you have lost the best friend you ever had in life.'

They took their journey homewards, the young women by far too much engrossed by their own future to pay heed to the wise man's parting words to the child, or speculate upon what they could mean. Sally was promised a new doll if she held her tongue.

Esther J.'s gate was the first reached, and she passed through it. Phillis and Sally D. went on to their own house : which they found full of distress and confusion. Their father was dead. The farmer had dropped down that morning in a fit of apoplexy. Poor little Sally had indeed lost her best friend in life—her father.

Now the reader must make the best and the worst that he can of this. It is strictly true.

Mr. Juniper did not know what to make of it. He was at the farm when the daughters got in, having been the medical man sent for : and Phillis, beside herself with excitement and grief, repeated to him what the Wizard had said to the child. Mr.

Juniper considered it strange. It might, of course, have been only a saying at hazard curiously fulfilled. The only other solution he could think of was—that the Wizard must in some way (there had been time) have heard of Farmer D.'s death : yet this seemed unlikely. Some other unaccountable sayings of the man had previously become known to Mr. Juniper, and he determined to pay him a visit the following week. But, as already stated, he went too late ; the man was gone.

Louis de Courcy never flirted with Georgy Juniper again ; from that hour he was a wiser and a graver man. The death of the ill-fated Florence had its effect upon all, and henceforward the girls were less careless, more staid and sober. Georgiana married in the course of years, and went over the seas with her husband ; and poor Cicely's wedding never came at all.

Her sisters, one after another, quitted the parent home ; but she was left. And in latter years Cicely grew to think her own life was the happiest, for it was free from care.

Never again was the Wizard heard of in Worcester. Whence he had derived his information, that spirit of divination which he really appeared to possess, none could, or did, pretend to speculate—for indeed this record of him has been no fancy sketch. Those who were living at the time, witnesses to the stir he caused, are dead and gone ; and a few of a later generation remain yet in Worcester to retain remembrance of the Chronicle.

'FLOREAT SEMPER FIDELIS CIVITAS.'

THE UNHOLY WISH

171

PART THE FIRST.

I.

It had been a lovely day for the season—
October: and the slanting beams of the
evening sun fell on one of our fair English
scenes. The pretty village of Ebury, with
its long straggling street, lay in a hollow;
its church and graveyard flanking it at one
end, a large white villa standing at the
other. Beyond and around extended a
goodly landscape; woods and dales, smiling
green plains and rippling streams, fields
from which the grain had been carried;
farmhouses dotted about, with a goodly
mansion here and there; while almost at
hand, a mile off, say, rose the chimneys and

walls of Ebury Hall, the residence of Squire Hardwick.

Leaning over the small iron gate that gave admittance to the lawn and flower-beds in front of the white villa, was a girl in the sweet springtime of early womanhood —Miss Emily Bell. The setting sun shone upon her, lighting up her face and the becoming simplicity of the dress she wore, a summer muslin sprigged with pink—for the days of monstrosities in the shape of attire had not come in by many a year.

About twelve months before, this house, empty then and to be let on lease, had been taken by a stranger from London, a Mr. Bell. Of course Ebury, being one of our aristocratic country places, at once began to question who and what Mr. Bell was, or had been. It was soon known that he had been a member of the Stock Exchange, and had made his fortune.

Ebury idlers flocked to call upon them at the white villa. They found Mr. Bell a companionable, intelligent man, Mrs. Bell a quiet, delicate woman, and Miss Emily, the eldest of six children, a very charming girl. Mr. Bell went up to London for two days every week, to attend the meetings of a bank of which he had become director, which left Miss Emily more at liberty to follow her own devices, as regarded the flirtations with her various admirers.

Lingering at the gate this evening, her eyes went roving down the short avenue to the high road that crossed it, as though looking for anything that might pass along. She had not long to wait. There loomed slowly into view the large, high phaeton of Squire Hardwick, the Squire driving, a gentle, pleasing girl sitting beside him, his only daughter, and a groom in the handsome Hardwick livery attending them. The Squire had drawn up his horses to a walking pace, the better to talk to a young man whom he had overtaken in the road. This was James Ailsa, a slender, gentlemanly, honest-hearted young doctor of four-and-twenty years, who had come to Ebury some months before to temporarily assist Mr. Winnington. Emily Bell, watching them go by, did not seem to like the sight.

'What a shame!' she cried. 'She's *always* talking to him!'

'Emily,' called out a voice at this moment, that of her sister Margaret, from one of the windows, 'do you not know we are at tea? Mamma says you are to come in at once.' And, when the very last lingering sound of the phaeton wheels had died away, Emily Bell turned from the gate and crossed the lawn to obey.

She was certainly a wondrously pretty girl—and she knew it—with her brown glossy hair, the damask colour of her cheeks, and her laughing eyes, dark as an April violet. As to her figure, it was for ever being compared to all things that were light and beautiful, a sylph and the Venus di Medicis; but to those who had really *seen* Medicis' goddess, the former comparison appeared by far the more suitable.

But what a flirt was she!—and how greedy of admiration! How many lovers had she drawn into her net only since she had come to Ebury? First, there was Mr. Grey, a handsome young fellow who came down for the shooting season; next followed young Campbell, an out-and-out flirt himself; then came the sentimental walks with that tall college man, who was reading with the Reverend Mr. Tuck's curate—much reading he did! no wonder he got plucked in his Little Go; and now for some time past it had been James Ailsa. And all these without reckoning Tom Hardwick, who had been her admirer, in an off-hand manner, all along.

It was a great pity James Ailsa fell so madly in love with her. He was told to beware of her blandishments, and how she would probably serve him; how many she had already loved, or professed to love; and then thrown them coolly off. But the warning came too late. Besides, he did not believe it : to him she seemed an angel upon earth, and he could not credit aught against her. In face and manner and speech she was of those sweetly innocent girls who take men's hearts by storm. There are such girls, as their victims know to their cost. No, he would believe nothing. So the young doctor was left to his fate, and to the seductions cf Miss Bell.

It could have been only for amusement that Emily began the flirtation : he was a quiet, retiring man, attractive in person and manners ; but as to anything serious, his position, with *her* high notions, would forbid that—a surgeon's assistant, and without prospects. It was understood that he had no money, and was quite friendless ; so many of those who had money, and influential friends also, rather slighted him, Tom Hardwick for one.

Mr. Tom Hardwick—the name was pronounced Hardick, and some people wrote it so—was the second son of the Squire, and had a fortune in his own right. He was the fashion at Ebury ; the village beholding with indescribable admiration his daring feats and scrapes, his lavish expenditure of money, his blood horses, his scarlet hunting-coats. His time was passed in fox-hunting, steeple-chasing, horse-racing, dog-fighting, boating,

shooting, and so on : and, although Miss
Emily Bell chose to favour him, she was not
in love with him. But, wanting good
birth herself, she looked up to the house
of Hardwick, who traced its pedigree back
to royalty and was connected with some of
the best county families, with undue reverence. Hence chiefly arose her patronage of
Mr. Tom ; and never better pleased was she
than when strolling through the village with
that gentleman talking nonsense at her side,
the village rustics bowing and curtseying to
him at every step : marks of respect which
Mr. Tom would carelessly acknowledge or
wholly neglect, according to the leisure his
gallant speeches to Emily allowed him.

The morning following the evening
above spoken of, Emily Bell left the break-
fast-table and retired to her own chamber,
fastening the door after her. She then un-
locked a small cabinet, which formed the

middle of a low, old-fashioned walnut-tree set of drawers, and drew forth a bundle of letters. They were from James Ailsa. Other packets were there, tied up with blue, pink, or yellow ribbon, and were the epistles of former lovers, but those Emily did not disturb. She opened three or four of James Ailsa's, glancing at their contents here and there : and we may do so with her. She was fond of reading over his letters, they spoke of passion so true and deep. Probably she cared for the writer more than she admitted to herself.

' Oh, thank, thank you ! to the last hour of my life will I thank you : whatever may be the fate of my love, and whether it shall hereafter be accepted or rejected, still will I thank and bless you. Your little note has relieved me from suspense almost intolerable. A thousand fears were in my heart ; a dread, almost as of death, was on my soul, that you might indignantly spurn me, and fling back my letter with scorn.

'Do you remember, Emily, that morning a few weeks ago, when we were walking together on the Brenton road, and our conversation turned on the subject of love? Do you recollect how confused I became, breaking off in the middle of a sentence, and that after an interval of silence I dropped the topic for another? Can you guess the cause of that embarrassment?— did you guess it then? That my passion for you was so great I could not speak on the subject of love to you without the most painful agitation—without betraying more than I then dared.'

This is an extract from another :

'Oh, Emily, dearest Emily, how can I support the rapture which has throbbed within me since last night? You confessed I was not indifferent to you—your head for

a few moments was pillowed on my bosom
—those kisses which I snatched still seem
to linger on my lips. I did not attempt to
go to rest; it would have been useless; I
sat in my room and watched the stars till
morning. I lived over and over again our
interview. I dared to conjure up visions of
the future, *our* future. I pressed my hands
to my temples, and asked if this taste of
paradise were not a dream. I ask it still.
I repeat to myself, " She loves, she loves
me! " Ought not our lives to be one continued breath of thanksgiving to Heaven for
having given us the power to taste on earth
such all-perfect bliss? '

Here follows another :

' Why, my love, do you mention fore-
bodings so gloomy?—Why should we sepa-
rate? It is true my position now is not
such as would warrant my demanding you
of your father; but, Emily, *know you not*

what such love as mine can dare to plan and effect? Rely upon it, though we see not the means yet, my fate in life shall not be an obscure one—it *shall* be such as to justify my asking you to share it.'

Then this :

' Emily, Emily, I am tortured nearly to madness.   You tell me you do not like Hardwick : then why show him these marks of favour ?   Last night, when we left, I was close to you ; my arm was ready ; yet you passed me and took his.   It cannot be that you did not see me : or if you did not see me, you do not love.   *I* look for *you :* I see but you : at a distance, before another's eyes could possibly distinguish your form, my heart tells me it is you.   Oh, Emily, if your love were but a tithe of what mine is, you could not so act.'

And this extract is from the last letter she had received from him :

'Forgive, forgive me, my only love. I did not mean to reproach you : I will believe, Emily, I am too exacting. I will believe, no one knows how willingly, that your heart is wholly mine. But if you knew how I love, what I suffer for you, you would not wonder that I cannot bear even the semblance of an attachment to another.'

Emily sat contemplating the characters of this last letter, and a smile and a blush stole over her face. Were they the tokens of love, or only of triumphant vanity ?

Presently she reached her writing materials, and began a note to Ailsa, 'My dearest James.' Whilst thus occupied, some one tried the door of the room, and, finding it fastened, knocked loudly against it. Emily scuffled all signs of her employment away.

'What do you want now ? ' she pettishly

asked, admitting her sister, vexed at being interrupted.

'What do I want!' repeated Margaret, resenting the question. 'The room is as much mine as it is yours; I may come into it when I please. Look here, Emily; Tom Hardwick is downstairs. He has brought an invitation from Mary for us to join them in a picnic to-day; they have visitors at the Hall, and are at a loss for amusement.'

'*That* is not Hardwick's voice!' exclaimed Emily, listening.

'That is James Ailsa's. Tom Hardwick is in the drawing-room with mamma,' answered Margaret. 'Ailsa has come up to see baby. Mind you don't tell *him* about the picnic, Emily, or we shall have him pushing himself into it.'

'You are more likely to tell him than I am,' cried Emily, as she ran downstairs.

Mr. Ailsa was in the hall. His pale,

sweet-tempered countenance lighted up as he advanced to greet Emily.

'James,' she whispered, as he threw his arm round her for a momentary embrace, while they were yet alone, 'do you know anything of the party they are planning for to-day?'

'What party, my love?'

'Some picnic of Mary Hardwick's. Will you come to it?'

'I have no invitation.'

'Nonsense about an invitation. It is in the open air, you know, and you can join us as if by accident. James, you must come.'

'I will brave all for you, Emily,' was his answer. 'They have called me an intruder —a thruster forward of myself. No matter; the comments and ill-natured remarks of the world fall on my heart as the idle wind whilst I have the consciousness of your love to make its sunshine.'

II.

' I DO believe that is James Ailsa coming along ! ' exclaimed Miss Margaret Bell, as the merry party were gathered à-la-gipsy on the outskirts of Beech Wood. 'Who can have told him we were here ? '

'Oh, he ferrets out our plans himself,' retorted Tom Hardwick ; 'he has the deuce's luck and his own too at that underhand fun. Treat him with the contempt he deserves, all of you, and don't speak to him ; do you hear, Mary ? '

Mary Hardwick heard, but she possessed too much good feeling and sense to heed her brother's counsels. James Ailsa was a thorough gentleman, except perhaps in pocket, and that he was not so regarded by everyone was only owing to Mr. Tom Hardwick's incessant ridicule and abuse of him. Tom Hardwick was as inferior to Ailsa as one man can well be to another; but people are ever ready to take part with the great and powerful, and Mr. Tom Hardwick held sway at Ebury.

Ailsa came up, and, after greeting the circle, was invited by Miss Hardwick, somewhat timidly, to sit down and join them.

'Enjoying a stroll in the woods this fine day, and so popped upon us unawares?' broke in Tom Hardwick, in a sarcastic tone.

'I am on my way to pay a visit to Mrs. Hudson,' answered Ailsa. And he spoke truth.

'Then you have come a precious deal out of your way,' retorted Hardwick, coarsely. 'It is nearer to go by the road.'

'I was going by the road,' returned

Ailsa, ' but crossed the field on seeing you here.'

He looked at Emily, seeking for a glance to recompense him for the painful position to which, for her sake, he had subjected himself, sensitive and unobtrusive as he was by nature ; but he looked in vain. The ban was on him—he was a despised man ; and Emily—proud, vain, and little-minded— followed the example around her, and noticed him not. Miss Hardwick felt deeply for his situation, and she talked to him pleasantly and offered him cake and wine—which he declined. Presently he rose from his seat to pursue his way. Mary Hardwick asked him if he would come to the Hall in the evening ; they should probably be having a little dance. He thanked her, and accepted.

The others were leaving their places to disperse about the wood.

' Emily must have told him we should

be here,' exclaimed Margaret Bell to Tom Hardwick, who was standing with his back against a tree, ' for as to his seeing us from the road, it's all stuff.'

' A lie,' uttered Mr. Tom, politely. ' If he had ten telescopes, and set 'em all up in a line, he could not see over to Beech Wood.'

' Emily pretends to dislike and despise him, but I saw——'

' As to my sister Mary, she's turning daft, I think—encouraging the fellow as she does.'

' I saw him kiss Emily the other day, and slip a letter into her hand,' continued Margaret, unheeding the interruption.

' You had better take care what you say,' exclaimed Tom Hardwick, growing very red in the face.

' It is truth,' answered the young lady. ' I was peeping at them through the green-house window.'

' Does he often write to her ?   Does she

write to him?' asked Tom, quite purple with rage.

'*I* can't tell whether she writes to him,' said Margaret, 'but she is always locking herself in our bedroom, and two or three times I have looked through the keyhole, and seen her scuffling the ink away. Don't you tell her I said this.'

'Oh, bother!' answered the gallant gentleman, 'I'll have it all out at once, one way or the other. Where is she now?'

Upon James Ailsa's leaving he struck through the wood path, his nearest way then, to Mrs. Hudson's house. But scarcely had he gone many steps when Emily stole after him, and called him, softly, by name. He turned and met her.

'James,' she whispered, 'are you going to stay with us?'

'*Am I going to stay!*' he replied, laying a painful stress upon every word. 'Emily,

if your heart can truly say that it wishes me
to do so, I will; and bear in silence.'

'Dear, dear James,' she said, tears rising
to her eyes, 'why do you speak to me
in so cold a tone—why do you look so
reproachfully at me?'

'Have I not cause?' he rejoined, painfully
excited; but even then he gave way to his
enduring love, and clasped her hands ten-
derly in his.

'Why do you permit Hardwick to appear
on these most familiar terms with you?' he
remonstrated. 'To all but me he must be
looked upon as your lover.'

'James,' she said earnestly, raising her
head from his shoulder, where it had been
lying, 'indeed you need not be jealous of
him. I have no love for Tom Hardwick; I
have scarcely any liking for him. Believe
me, dear, dear James.'

He did not answer; but he pressed his

burning forehead upon hers. She felt its throbbing.

At this moment the voice of Mr. Tom Hardwick was heard. Emily started from her lover; and, pressing his hand in token of farewell, stole silently away amongst the trees.

'Who is that in the wood, Emily?' exclaimed Tom Hardwick, as she emerged from it. 'I heard voices.'

'The wind, perhaps,' returned Emily, carelessly. 'Or—I was humming a tune to myself; you may have heard that.'

'Don't trouble yourself with any more falsehoods,' rejoined Hardwick, dashing into the subject without ceremony; 'you were talking with that presuming fool, Ailsa. And as I don't mean to stand this nonsense about him any longer, I shall acquaint Mr. Bell with the fact that you and he have been writing love-letters to each other.'

'Oh, for Heaven's sake, say nothing to my father!' cried Emily, well-nigh startled out of her senses.

'I am glad you have the grace not to deny it,' interrupted Hardwick sullenly.

'Yes, yes, yes,' exclaimed the agitated girl, striving to repair the unlucky admission she had made: 'I do deny it.'

'Emily, I will not be trifled with, so you may spare yourself the attempt. You shall either promise to be mine, and keep to it, or I will give you up at once.'

This was the nearest approach to an offer Emily had ever received from Mr. Tom Hardwick, and she felt somewhat overpowered with bewildering sensations. On the one hand was James Ailsa, with his steadfast love, which she knew would shield her from every harm in life; on the other was the tempting prospect of becoming a daughter-in-law of the lofty old squire; and this last was irresistible to her aspiring heart.

'It shall be one of us, not both,' resumed Hardwick, who was in an ill-humour, and a very resolute one: and little did Emily guess that he had no intention whatever of marrying her or anyone else; for he could not afford it. 'And here I swear,' continued he, 'that if you ever again attempt to speak to that beggar, Ailsa, I will take no further notice of you whatever: if we meet in the streets I'll pass you; should you call at my father's house, I will go out of it whilst you are there.'

'Oh, Tom, why do you put yourself into this dreadful passion? I declare to you that I hate James Ailsa.'

'Then you will deliver up his letters to Mr. Bell.'

'For the love of goodness, don't mention the subject to papa,' she implored; 'he is so strict with us. He *has* written me one or two nonsensical letters, I won't deny it. I will give them up to you, Tom, if you will not tell papa. But you won't read them?'

'Not I. I'll make them into a packet, and dash it into Ailsa's face.'

'Don't talk so wildly, Tom: you know Ailsa is no coward. If you want to get up a quarrel, I will have nothing more to say to you, any more than to him; and I will keep the letters.'

'Well, well, Emily, I'll promise you to let the beggar alone; and he shall know nothing about the letters. I shall come for them to-morrow morning, mind.'

'Very well,' said Emily, deep in thought.

'There's my darling girl,' he added, stooping to salute her cheek; 'and when I can afford to marry, you shall be my wife.'

Emily made no reply to this exceedingly

gracious promise. She was thinking what excuse she could make about the letters, for as to giving them up to him, that she was determined never to do. 'Who in the world can have told him that we correspond?' she soliloquised. 'If it should come to be known in Ebury, I think I shall go mad—everyone so despises Ailsa. If Tom Hardwick had sent me love-letters now, I should not care who knew it: they might take and publish them in the newspapers if they liked.'

The carpet-dance took place that evening at the Hall; but James Ailsa did not appear at it. He was some miles away, attending upon one of Mr. Winnington's patients. With the morning, Mr. Tom Hardwick arrived at the white villa, according to his promise. Emily met him on the lawn.

'Oh, is it you!' she exclaimed, as if surprised.

'I said I should be here early,' he answered. ' I have come for the letters.'

' The letters!—oh, I have destroyed them.'

' You have done *what?* ' he asked.

' I feared you might send them to Ailsa, as you threatened,' she said, ' so I thought it safer to burn them.'

' It is a lie! ' exclaimed Hardwick, angered out of his good manners. ' Emily, I am not to be done in this way. Give me the letters, or, by my honour, I will go straight to your father.'

' I *have* destroyed them,' she replied tremblingly. ' I thought it the wisest and safest plan. It is of no use being angry, the thing is done. But for the future, Tom, you may trust me, for may I never stir from here if I don't hate James Ailsa; and I'll never speak to him again.'

What further romancing might have been

indulged in by Emily was cut short by her mother's calling to her; so she ran in, leaving Mr. Tom Hardwick standing where he was.

'Will you walk in?' called out Mrs. Bell to him.

'No, I thank you,' he answered sullenly.

And, turning away, he had not left the gates many minutes when he encountered Mr. Bell.

'Good-morning, Mr. Tom. All well at home, I hope.'

'I was coming in search of you, sir,' said Hardwick, speaking in a very excited manner, and taking no notice of Mr. Bell's salutation. 'An unpleasant matter has come to my knowledge, which I think you ought to be made acquainted with. That upstart, penniless fellow, Ailsa, has taken upon himself to make love to your daughter, and, unless a check is administered to him, he may be drawing her into a mess ; a promise to marry him, or some such madness. Girls are such simpletons.'

'My daughter?—Emily?' cried the astonished man.

'Emily, of course. He has been sending her love-letters. She has a whole heap of them, I daresay.'

'Take care what you do say, sir,' advised Mr. Bell.

'Oh, it is quite correct, I assure you, sir. I thought I would give you a hint of what vas going on,' continued the friendly Tom, 'and do as I would be done by. If it were my sister, for instance, I should hold myself under eternal obligations to the man who had enlightened *me*. There's no harm in love-letters, of course, when they come from the right man. But Ailsa is just——'

'Thanks, thanks, my dear Mr. Hardwick,' exclaimed Mr. Bell, wringing his hand, and

tearing indoors at a great rate, too much
excited to listen further.

Emily was in her bedroom, having taken
refuge there until Tom Hardwick should be
safely gone. When she saw her father enter,
instinct told her that something was wrong.
Shutting the door, he, in a voice that spoke
of suppressed passion, asked for the letters
which she had received from James Ailsa.

The startled girl stood transfixed before
him : every vestige of colour forsook her
countenance; the sickness of terror flew to
her heart.

'Do you hear me, disgraceful girl?' resumed Mr. Bell, who was very strict with
his daughters, and had believed them to be
models of good behaviour. 'Give me the
letters without trouble, or I will open your
places and search for them myself.'

It was too stern a moment for equivoca-
tion. Emily faltered out that they were

there, and pointed with her hand to the cabinet in the chest of drawers. It was safely locked.

'Produce them.'

She stood still as a post.

'Produce them,' repeated her father.

She shivered and trembled, holding the back of a chair for support; but she opened the cabinet and took out the letters. Above them lay the epistle she had begun to Ailsa the previous morning, and had thrust away in her haste when interrupted by her sister. It of course came forth with the others, but Emily, hoping she was not observed, pushed it back.

'What paper is that?' cried Mr. Bell. 'What are you trying to put back?'

She faltered out something about 'some poetry.'

'Give it to me with the rest, Emily; how dare you attempt to trifle with me? You may have your poetry again when I have looked at it—if it is poetry.'

He took it, with the letters, from her hand, and the first words that caught his gaze were, 'My dearest James.' Two or three lines of little import followed—the cream of Emily's letters was seldom at the beginning. Mr. Bell tore the paper into the smallest particles, and with a glance of un-utterable rage at Emily, advanced to the window and scattered them to the winds.

'Are these all?' he demanded, pointing to the packet of letters which he held in his hand.

'Yes; all,' faltered Emily.

'Open the cabinet again, that I may see for myself,' returned Mr. Bell. 'I cannot trust you.'

'Papa,' she cried, clasping her hands in terror, lest he should execute his threat, and so find that Mr. James Ailsa had not been her first correspondent in the love-letter line, 'on my word, on my honour they are all. I never received so much as a sentence or a scrap of paper from him besides. The letters themselves will prove that they are all.'

It was impossible to doubt that she spoke the truth, and Mr. Bell stalked out of the room with the letters in his hand. Emily sank into a chair and sobbed aloud.

Somehow or other, all this gossip went forth to the public, and with innumerable exaggerations. Also the account of Mr. Bell's stormy interview with James Ailsa, when the latter was compelled to give up Emily's letters to him, in the midst of some contemptuous taunts at a paltry, penniless surgeon's assistant presuming to think of Miss Emily Bell. That James Ailsa, sensitive and shrinking, did not repose just then upon a bed of roses may be easily understood.

The next news Ebury heard was that Ailsa—but there's something to relate first. ·

It was one of the most wretched nights that November ever turned out—cold, rainy, and boisterous. A light shone in the curtained window of Emily Bell's chamber; she herself was there, wretched as the weather, having been ordered, ever since the explosion, to keep within it. This was a severe punishment for Emily, whose whole existence lay in the exercise of her flirting talents. She was sitting dull enough, in a low rocking-chair, which she had fetched out of the nursery, swaying herself backwards and forwards, wishing bedtime had come, when Margaret would be up, or that the term of her punishment was at an end, when a rattling at the window, as of gravel thrown at it, made her start from her chair. A few moments, and the summons was repeated, so she softly opened the window.

'It is James Ailsa,' whispered her heart. He drew close under the window, and asked her to come down to him for a few moments.

'What a request, James!'

'It is the last I shall have to make you,' he said. 'I am going away for ever.'

'You are joking.'

'The last few days have been no joke for me,' he answered, 'or such as to incline me to joking. I repeat to you, Emily, that I am going; and it may be that this is our last meeting on earth.'

She left the window, and, stealing down the stairs, ran out at a back door, and so round the house until she came in sight of James. He drew her underneath some trees, where they were shielded from observation, and partially so from the pouring rain.

'James,' she said, 'I am doing very wrong in thus coming down to you, because you know our intimacy is at an end.'

'I do know it,' he replied bitterly, 'and it is not for the purpose of clandestinely inducing you to renew it, or to act contrary to the wish of your parents, that I am here.'

Emily, arrant flirt that she was, felt rather disappointed, for she had fancied Mr. James's nocturnal visit *had* that tendency, and would have experienced much gratification in refusing the boon; or, to speak more correctly, in being asked it.

'Hear me,' said Ailsa. 'I have loved you, Emily, with no common love: few have loved another in this world as I love you. If you possess the same affection for me, any fate will be more tolerable to you than hopeless separation; and the very thought of marrying another must be hateful to you. Now listen. I would not fetter you by word or deed; but if your heart will whisper one hope to me, I shall go forth a different man : life will be as bright to me as all is now dark.'

'I do not understand you,' replied Emily. 'We are separated, therefore what hope can I give you?'

'The hope that when my efforts have been crowned with success; when I shall have acquired fame, fortune, that even you might be proud to share, I may return and woo you.'

'It is so long to look forward to!' was her answer, delivered in a grumbling tone.

'That is sufficient,' returned Ailsa sadly. 'It has convinced me of what I feared.' And, had the light permitted, Emily might have seen the despair that stole to his countenance; but she could not have seen it, in all its bitter sickness, as it then and there seated itself upon his heart. 'Had you put the question to me,' he continued, 'and required me to wait until our hairs were grey, and our steps feeble, I should have knelt and blessed you. Did you love as I love, this request of mine would have made a heaven of your days; it would have held forth a hope to cheer the whole of existence.'

'But what would papa say? He——'

'I think you do not quite understand me,' interrupted Ailsa, in the same tone of sadness, which indeed characterised his conversation and manner through the entire interview: 'I said I would not fetter you—I would not encourage an act rebellious to your parents. But the secret feelings of the heart cannot be controlled or hindered, even at the command of those we are bound to obey, and I knew that if your misery were what mine is—in thus speaking to you—— no matter.'

He stopped; he was greatly agitated.

'You take things too much to heart, James.'

'I will not do so in future,' he exclaimed, almost vehemently. 'In the years to come, I will struggle with all my dearest feelings, and uproot them, one by one. I must struggle to uproot your image, Emily, which has entwined itself round my very heartstrings. Heaven knows it will be a bitter task.'

'But if I were to give you this promise——'

'I did not ask for a promise,' he interrupted.

'Well, this hope then: it would be of little use; it is not like a regular engagement.'

'It is too late—I do not ask it now,' he hastily answered, 'for it would be valueless, unless precious to you as to me. I thought perhaps it might have been so; against my fears and my better judgment I thought so.'

'I fancy, James, these dreams of yours,

about fame and fortune, are very chimerical,'
was her next remark.

'They may prove so now,' he answered,
'wanting the spur that would have urged
them on to realisation.'

'I am sure I wish I could see you rise
to—to—to be Physician to the Queen.'

'I have now only to take my leave of
you,' he said, leaving her wild, and perhaps
not very sincere, thought unanswered.

'But why do you go away, James, in
this hasty manner? Where do you propose
going?'

'Anywhere. I have no plans. No
matter what part of the globe I am in,
so that it be not Ebury. I—I—heard a
rumour to-day—I heard the same yesterday,' he continued, jerking his sentences out,
as if in too much agitation to speak in even
periods: 'that I am given up for Mr. Tom
Hardwick.'

'It is not true,' she exclaimed fiercely; but Ailsa shook his head.

'Why did Tom Hardwick interfere between us, Emily?—why should he, of all people, make it his business to seek your father, and tell him that I loved you? And you, why should you have promised to give up my letters to him?'

'Who told you that?' cried Emily, her face in a glow.

'I gathered it from his own foolish boasting; from the unjustifiable remarks he made in the presence of your father, for the few minutes that during our interview he was present. They had might on their side; while *I*——'

'No one ever believes half Tom Hardwick says,' she stammered. 'And I declare to you, James, that I hate the sight of him.'

'You are flattered by his attentions because his family is good and he holds some sway in the neighbourhood,' resumed Ailsa; 'but these recommendations are only negative. They will not compensate for qualities that he lacks; and beware, Emily, lest in looking after the shadow you lose the substance.'

'You need not give me this advice, James; I tell you Tom Hardwick is nothing to me.'

'Farewell, Emily,' he murmured, wringing her hands. 'You know not the value of the heart you have rejected; the spirit you have broken. Be assured that few men love as I have loved. I would have guarded you in my bosom; shielded you from harm; warded from you unhappiness. May the husband you shall choose cherish you as I would have done. Farewell.'

She burst into tears, and laid her head upon his shoulder, as formerly. But the passionate embrace that would once have rewarded her was withheld now—with violence to his own feelings, but still withheld. He knew now that she did not love him; at least with a love worthy to mate with such as his.

'Farewell, Emily,' he repeated, as he raised her gently, when the paroxysm of her emotion was over; and, with another wring of the hand, he was gone.

As James Ailsa gained the road from the short avenue he came upon Miss Hardwick. Attended by a servant, she was on her way to spend the evening with some friends. She stopped when she saw him.

'Is this true, Mr. Ailsa?' she asked, in her soft, gentle voice—'that you are quitting Ebury?'

'Quite true,' he answered.

'But why?'

'Ebury has not treated me altogether

well on the whole,' he answered, after a
pause. 'I do not care to remain in it.'

'We shall be sorry.'

'No, no; not anyone will be sorry for
me. At least, scarcely anyone. Let me
say "Good-bye" to you now, dear Miss
Hardwick, and thank you—thank *you*—for
all the considerate kindness that you have
ever shown me.'

Tears filled Mary Hardwick's eyes; it
was dark, and he did not see them. And,
their hands lingering together in a warm
pressure, they parted.

James Ailsa, scarcely conscious of what
he was about, turned into the plantation
that flanked one side of Mr. Bell's house,
dwelling upon his recent parting with Emily.
His misery was great; far greater than they
can form any idea of who have not gone
through a similar ordeal. In the full sunshine of his love, he had once thanked

Heaven for bestowing upon us the power to taste of such unutterable bliss; he might now be grateful for the strength that enables us to support and *survive* its contrast.

The events of the last few days had been a severe trial to him, but what were they compared with that night's interview, when the conviction that she had never loved him forced itself upon his soul? He pressed his brow upon the rough bark of the trees; he walked hither and thither without aim; the weather was uncared for in his agony of mind; the hours also elapsed unheeded. But at length he was drenched to the skin, and began slowly to make his way home. The church clock was striking twelve as he reached Mr. Winnington's door.

He had forgotten his latch-key, and knocked gently, but the knock was unanswered; and in looking up at the house, no

light was to be seen: the curtains were
drawn closely before the windows, and total
silence prevailed. Everything seemed to
intimate that the family and servants were
in bed; and he, unwilling to disturb them,
and caring little, in his present frame of
mind, what became of him, retraced his
steps and walked about until morning. Soon
after twelve o'clock the rain had ceased, but
the wind continued boisterously high. His
frame shivered and shook with cold, but it
remained uncared for.

It was about half-past seven in the morning when he again waited at the door of the
surgeon's house, which stood in the middle
of the long street, and at the same moment
a horse was heard advancing at a brisk trot
from round the corner. Mechanically Ailsa
turned his eyes towards the sound.

It was Mr. Tom Hardwick, booted and
spurred, and trimly attired. He was going

to the steeplechase, full of congratulation that the wretched night had turned out so fine a morning. He saw James Ailsa standing there, and looked full at him, but did not condescend to speak. A gesture of contempt, not noticeable perhaps by one uninterested, but strangely · conspicuous to Ailsa, escaped him. Drawing his back proudly in and his head up, with unsuppressed triumph, he averted his eyes from his outwitted rival and rode on.

James Ailsa was stung almost into madness by the haughty glance and consciously triumphant bearing, and spoke passionate words aloud as he looked after him.

' I wish to God he may break his back ! '

Tom Hardwick, followed by his groom, continued his way to the Crown and Thistle, an inn situated about two miles from Ebury, and close to the ground marked out for the steeplechase. Here he found some friends awaiting him, and more were assembling, steeplechasers like himself, those to be engaged in the day's contest having agreed to breakfast there, with a select assemblage of supporters. The horses had been sent on the previous day.

This steeplechase had been a long-looked-for event, not only by Mr. Tom Hardwick and his sporting friends, but by the neighbourhood in general. Everyone had something staked on the great event, from the old squire's cool thousand, to Miss Emily Bell's pair of gloves. But the interest it excited, above that of all other steeple-chases, past or to come, was caused by the dangerous nature of the ground to be run over. None, save men deep in their cups, as had been the case in this affair, would have been so wild as to fix upon it. Five horses were to run, their owners to ride.

Six men had been at the convivial meeting,
whence the scheme had its origin, but one,
young James Gaunt, had in the meantime
gone to London, and was now lying there
dangerously ill. Many a one, after survey-
ing the ground, turned away with a shrug
of the shoulders, wondering if the parties
were already tired of life. Earl Dunnely,
the old lord-lieutenant of the county and
father of Viscount Chiselem, came in haste
from one of his distant seats, to endeavour
to prevail upon his son to renounce the
danger. But the young sporting men
thought it looked bravely fine to persist in
their contempt for the danger, and would
listen to nobody.

Viscount Chiselem's Daylight, Honourable Charles Easthope's Tartar, Mr. T.
Hardwick's Fire-and-fly, Mr. Prynn's Brown
John, Captain Flanagan's Cut-and-come-
again. Of these horses, Tartar was the

favourite, and most bets were laid on him—
except with the ladies. They, according to
custom, only saw the merits of the horses
through the attractions of their riders, and
their little betting was free enough upon
the *gentlemen* favourites, these being, very
generally, Lord Chiselem and Mr. Tom
Hardwick. Emily Bell's gloves were of
course red-hot upon Fire-and-fly.

III.

EVERYONE had gone to the steeplechase, man, woman, and child ; not a soul was left at home to take care of the village, which might have run away with itself without hindrance. Even Miss Emily Bell, in spite of her disgrace, had been conveyed thither by her parents in the hired carriage. They may have deemed it safer to take her than to leave her.

One exception there was, James Ailsa ; he was in no mood for steeplechases. His preparations for leaving Ebury were completed ; he was in haste to depart ; but he had promised Mr. Winnington to remain until the latter should return from the scene of the day's sport, to which he was about to drive his sister.

The gig waited at the door, and the good old surgeon, who was going on for sixty years, lingered in the surgery with Ailsa, expressing again, for the tenth time, his regret that James should leave him.

'I know you only came to me as a temporary thing when I was ill, James; I know that. But we have got on so well together that I had begun to hope you would have stayed with me always.'

James Ailsa sighed as he answered: 'Thank you for all your kind thoughts, dear Mr. Winnington, but it could not be. I cannot remain at Ebury.'

'Are you ready, Charles?' cried little Miss Winnington, putting her face, encased in its white curls, into the surgery; 'we shall be late.'

'Quite ready, Matty,' said the doctor cheerily; and they drove off together.

The morning wore on, wearily enough to James Ailsa; but at length he saw signs of people in the distance.

They were coming back at last, not one or two stragglers only, but in groups. Ailsa had been watching for them at the door a long time, and he stood and watched them still. A horseman clattered past riding as if for his life. It was the butler at the Hall. Following close upon him came another; and this proved to be young Chewton, the lawyer's son. He saw Ailsa, and pulled up.

' Have you been there, Ailsa? I did not see you.'

' No.'

' This is a horrible thing, is it not? '

'Has there been any accident?' demanded Ailsa.

'Oh, have you not heard? Tom Hardwick's killed.'

Ailsa, strong man as he was, shook in every limb.   He drew back and leaned against the door-post for support.

'Is he dead?' he gasped.

'He was not dead when I left,' replied young Chewton, 'but they say he cannot survive the night.   *His back is broken.*'

Ailsa shuddered, as if something super-natural were creeping over him.

'Why, Ailsa, the news has startled you indeed!   You are as white as a corpse.'

There was no reply.

'One would think you were going to faint,' continued Mr. Chewton.   'Can't you speak?   Are you insensible?'

At that moment he was, to all outward things.   A prayer was ascending from his heart to Heaven for forgiveness for the sinful wish he had that morning uttered as

Hardwick passed him, and which had been so strangely fulfilled.

'By the way, Easthope has got his arm smashed—or his leg; I forget which,' resumed Chewton.

'You forget which!'

'I really do. Minor accidents are lost sight of before such a calamity as Hardwick's. The poor horses, for instance—nobody has cast a thought towards them. Chiselem was thrown twice, and got stunned; and Flanagan was flung into Briar Pond. I don't know whether he's out yet.'

'But Tom Hardwick!' uttered Ailsa, incapable of listening to any other topic; 'I would sacrifice my own life to save his.'

'What a vain wish!' exclaimed Chewton. 'By the way, have you heard that James Gaunt's dead?'

'James Gaunt! was *he* there?'

'No, no; news came this morning to the Manor House. He died in town.'

'Oh, goodness me! there never was such a steeplechase before!' squeaked little Tuck, Mr. Winnington's new apprentice, as he ran up. 'Mamma need not have said I shouldn't go, for fear I should get a liking for steeplechases. I'll never go to another. It was dreadful, Mr. Ailsa. You should have heard Tom Hardwick's groans. If you please, sir, can they set a broken back?'

'Not exactly,' said young Chewton, answering for Ailsa, as he rode away.

Master Tuck was right. There never had been such a steeplechase before, at least within recollection. Lord Chiselem was thrown and picked up insensible; Mr. Easthope's shoulder was dislocated, and Tom Hardwick's back was broken. Two of the horses were killed, one was lamed, and another had disappeared altogether.

PART THE SECOND.

I.

IT was a very considerable time after Mr. Ailsa's departure, which, not having been announced previously to the general public, came upon Ebury as an electric shock, ere the steeplechase faded from its everyday thoughts. Indeed, it left behind it consequences to last as a memorial; rendering it, to the inhabitants, a sort of national event to date from, such as William of Normandy conquering England, the rebellion of Cromwell, or the murder of Perceval.

To the astonishment of all, Tom Hardwick did not die. He lay for many, many months in agony, and partially recovered, to remain a helpless cripple. In this suffering state he continued, hoping for no improvement on this side the grave, to whatever period his life might be prolonged. On fine days he was placed in a hand-carriage and drawn about the village—the once brilliant Tom. What a change! His old friends and associates would call in at his lodgings —for he had left the Hall, as will be seen— or walk by his side as he was drawn about, relating all the scraps of news they could pick up, to cheer his spirits. Emily Bell would often join him, though without hope of flirting—all idea of which for him, poor fellow, was at an end for ever. Neither did Emily herself seem to pursue the amusement so strenuously as before. Whether it was the sudden departure of James Ailsa that affected her spirits, or the accident to Tom, or that other young men were growing shy of her, could not be decided, but from about the time of the steeplechase very little was seen of Emily's flirtations.

Now it is very probable that what has further to be related of James Ailsa will appear too romantic to be true. The reader may say it will do for fiction; not for real life. But this tale *is* one of real life; as some of the actors in it, living yet, could testify. All its circumstances are simple facts, even to that rash and sinful wish of James Ailsa's, as his rival rode past him on the morning of the steeplechase, and its startling fulfilment.

Closely following upon Ailsa's departure, Mr. Winnington received a certain application from Sir John Gaunt. Sir John was lord of the manor of Ebury and the adjacent lands. He was owner, by purchase, of no inconsiderable portion of the village, the house occupied by the Bells forming part of it. Sir John Gaunt was a widower, and

had recently lost his son James, his only
child, a young man in the first bloom of
life. He had come of age only the year
before, which had been celebrated by re-
joicings at their residence, the Manor House
—little did anyone think then how soon his
course would be over. His name was down
to ride in the steeplechase, poor fellow, but
he did not live to see it run. Sir John had
himself long been in ill-health, and the grief
caused by his son's death augmented his dis-
order. His physicians ordered him to seek
change of scene in travel; and the purport
of his application to Mr. Winnington, who
was an old friend of his, was to inquire if
he knew any medical man who would accompany him as travelling companion and
medical attendant.

Mr. Winnington at once thought of
James Ailsa; he greatly esteemed and re-
spected him, and he knew that he could

most conscientiously recommend him to Sir
John Gaunt, as being in every way qualified
for the post. The old bachelor surgeon felt
indignant at the treatment Ailsa had received in Ebury ; perhaps he saw no objection to the writing of love-letters ; perhaps
he thought the whole blame lay with Miss
Bell, who had certainly began the flirtation herself, and had drawn Ailsa on. If
he and she must have been separated,
argued the doctor one day to a whole con-
clave of village gossips, it might have been
accomplished kindly and quietly, without all
that publicity and holding-forth of Ailsa to
general contempt and ridicule. Tom Hardwick's doing?—well, perhaps so ; it was
cruel enough, whosesoever doing it was. Not
that he would have had them marry off-
hand, confident of living upon air or practice
to come—no such thing. But they were
both young, and *might have waited.* Ailsa

was a clever man in his profession, and had years before him.

However, Mr. Winnington spoke in Ailsa's favour to Sir John Gaunt, who accepted the recommendation ; and, all pre- liminaries being arranged, they left England together.

The steeplechase killed one person, eventually, if not at the moment. Poor old Squire Hardwick, broken-hearted at the acci- dent to his favourite son, was, in less than six months afterwards, laid in his grave. And then came the change in Tom's fortunes. He had completely run through his own money ; the estates were entailed upon the eldest son, and the portion settled on the younger children was small. The Squire scraped together what he could for his un- fortunate son, which was not much, his reign having been too profuse and liberal to leave many resources at his command, and with his dying breath left him to the care of his heir. And that heir, so far as real assistance went, neglected the injunction.

Mr. Francis Hardwick, now the squire, took up his residence at the Hall. Since he had come of age he had chiefly lived away from it. Mary remained there as its mistress, for her brother was unmarried. It was still to be seen what sort of a life he would lead, whether a heedless and extravagant one, as his father and Tom had done, or one of a more rational description. Rumour said that he was close-handed ; but if so, quoth the village gossips, he was not a true Hardwick.

Ebury returned to its usual quietness— doubly quiet now that Mr. Tom Hardwick's freaks could not enliven it—and for some time nothing occurred worthy of note. It did at last, however. Mr. Bell got specu- lating with his money, and—as a natural sequence—turned it into ducks and drakes.

Ebury awoke one fine morning to find that Mr. Bell was ruined : nothing remained, it was understood, but the income of Mrs. Bell —a very small one. This sort of misfortune usually brings household affairs to a climax, and it did so with them. They sold off their furniture and departed for London, where Mr. Bell died.

For some years afterwards little was heard of them, but at that period Mr. Winnington, having a vacancy for an apprentice, wrote to Mrs. Bell, and offered, with a kindness of heart that did him honour, to take her youngest son without premium—an offer which was most thankfully accepted. In those days a boy intended for a surgeon began his studies as an apprentice. So the lad arrived at Ebury—a tall young shaver of fourteen : with a capacious forehead and lanky black hair.

Meanwhile, during these years, Sir John

Gaunt remained on the Continent, Ailsa always with him. Sir John could not bear the thought of returning to his desolate home. He had grown wonderfully attached to his companion, in whom from the first he saw, or fancied he saw, a resemblance to his lost son. The name, James, was also the same. But, apart from this, when he became thoroughly acquainted with Ailsa, it was impossible for him to be otherwise than attached to him.

Sir John struggled on with his incipient malady; sometimes he would be better, sometimes not; gradually, however, growing worse upon the whole, and at length he returned to England—to die. But he did not get further than London. Ailsa remained with him to the last—to part with him now would have been to Sir John almost like parting with life. That dread moment was not long in coming for him.

When Sir John Gaunt's will was opened, it was found he had left most substantial proof of his regard for Ailsa. All his property in the village of Ebury, consisting of houses and land, was bequeathed to him, with a considerable sum in money, and other property of value.

Now here was a strange thing. That young man, humble assistant to the country surgeon, had been driven from the village in contempt but seven years before, and now he returned to them a rich man, a landed proprietor, superior in position to most of those who had scorned him. In truth, it was passing strange.

It was as a dream to Ebury, or one of those electric shocks talked of before, when the house formerly occupied by the Bells was put into repair, preparatory to James Ailsa's taking up his residence there. All the village flocked to see the furniture

before its owner's arrival, from the Squire's
newly-married lady to good Miss Winnington's cook, who had grown old in
her service; for this romance in real life
stirred everyone, gentle and simple. Ailsa
had chosen it in London, and sent it down :
plain and unobtrusive it proved to be, to the
intense disappointment of the gaping visitors,
but with a quiet elegance pervading the
whole. But when James Ailsa first arrived
he went direct to the Manor House, where
he had business to transact and would
remain for a few days; being one of
the executors to the will. The Manor
House, with the rest of Sir John's property,
was left to a distant relative, the only one
he had. Ailsa was little altered, looking
scarcely, if any, older ; his pale complexion
was somewhat browned by travel, and his
manners were unassuming and gentlemanly
as usual. Not a whit of assumption or self-

consequence had his good fortune brought him.

In the afternoon of the second day, a cold one in January, he walked over to his own house, and spent an hour or two in looking round and about, giving directions for this and that to be altered or done. It was growing dusk when he went away. In the road, at the end of the avenue, a young lady was passing with a swift step in the direction of the village. They stopped simultaneously and their hands met.

'James!' she exclaimed.

And then Miss Hardwick, for she it was, blushed warmly.

'Mr. Ailsa, I meant,' she added; 'I beg your pardon.'

'Oh, don't do that!' he cried, almost with a touch of pain. 'If you only knew how grateful these little remembrances are to me! Why, do you know,' he continued, slightly laughing, 'I believe I was about to say, "Is it you, Mary!" boldly enough, you would have thought. Have you been quite well during all these years? You look thin.'

'All these years!' she repeated dreamily. 'Yes, it is more than seven years since you left.'

'You have kept count of them, then!'

Again Mary Hardwick blushed. 'My father died soon afterwards,' she said. 'I have kept count of the lapse of years since that.'

Their hands dropped apart; hitherto they had been linked together. 'It is rather curious,' remarked Ailsa, 'that we should meet upon precisely the same spot on which we parted. Do you remember?'

'Oh, yes. But not more strange than that you should come back to Ebury. I never thought you would do so.'

'Neither did I—then. Time changes our circumstances — and ourselves too. After the lapse of a few years we can hardly believe ourselves to be the same people that we were before. Ay, I have come back to the old place in my old days.'

Mary smiled.

'Indeed I feel old; very old compared with what I did when I left it. I am thirty-one.'

'And I am twenty-eight,' laughed Mary. '*That's* old, if you like, for a woman. But I must go,' she broke off; 'I am on my way to take tea with Miss Winnington.'

'I think I will walk with you, if you will allow me,' he said. 'I have not yet seen her, or my good old friend, her brother.'

So they turned away together.

And a few more weeks went on.

II.

IN the sitting-room of a small residence on the outskirts of London sat Mrs. Bell with her three daughters. She wore widow's weeds still, but the children were in colours.

It was the dusk of evening; and Emily was seated on a low stool, holding a letter in her hand, which she looked over by fire-light, sometimes laying it on her lap as if in thought, and then again recurring to it.

'I do think I should like to go, mamma,' she said at length. 'Mary, be quiet.'

'Read the letter to me again, Emily,' said Mrs. Bell. 'I only skimmed the heads of it this morning, I was so busy with the pudding, and I have had no time to look at

it since. Mary, my dear, you heard your
sister tell you to be quiet. Don't dance
about, but sit down and listen.'

Emily stirred the fire into a blaze, and
began to read :

'DEAR MAMMA,—I really did not think it
could have been five months since I wrote,
till your letter came to remind me last week,
and I am quite ashamed not to have answered your two last, and Miss Winnington
is very angry about it too ; but indeed, dear
mamma, I have been very busy lately. Mr.
Winnington says I get on very well. I bled
a person the other day ; it was that barber's
man round the corner; he who used to
be always drinking, you know. He fell
down in a fit close by our door, and they
brought him into the surgery. Mr. Winnington and Mr. Tuck were out, and I tried
the lancet and used it famously, and saved

the man's life. It's reckoned, I can assure
you, a great feather in my cap, down here.
I'm going into tooth-drawing next ; but that
requires muscle and nerve, and Mr. Tuck
says I am deficient in both at present. Mr.
and Miss Winnington are so kind ; what do
you think they did, mamma ? Because my
best clothes were getting shabby, they have
had a new suit made for me as a present—
such beauties ! But I think the trousers were
made out of some of Mr. Winnington's old
ones, for he used to wear a pair just like
them—grey stripes. I have a message
for you from Miss Winnington—won't it
make Emily dance ! She sends her respects
or love or something of that sort, and says
she wants to ask you a favour. It is that
you will send Emily to Ebury to visit her
for a month or two. She says the pleasant
springtime is close upon us, and she would
like her to come immediately. She begs

you to excuse her writing herself, because her eyes are so much dimmer than they were, but you are to write back to her in a week at furthest, and say which day Emily. will be with us. And Mr. Winnington says I am to tell you Emily shall be well taken care of, and that he will take no excuse. Do let her come, mamma.

'And now I have some news to tell you. Do you remember that Mr. Ailsa, when I was a little boy, who was with Mr. Winnington, and went travelling afterwards with Sir John Gaunt? Well, Sir John Gaunt is dead, and has left a fortune to Mr. Ailsa, money and houses, and heaps of things. He left him a carriage and a pair of horses—they are bays, so tall!—and lots of plate and books. Mr. Tuck says if it were him he should sell the musty old books, and he should buy a second pair of bays to match the others, and drive four-in hand. He thinks Mr. Ailsa would look first-rate with the ribbons in his hands, and four blood horses before him. And *our* old house is left to him, mamma, and Mr. Ailsa is come back here, and lives at it. It is done up beautifully, and he has made great improvements. I like Mr. Ailsa so much; he gave me half-a-sovereign on Easter Monday because it was a holiday. He does not forget, you see, that boys like to have something in their pockets on a holiday.

'I am sure Emily will find me grown. And tell her if she should want to be bled while she's here, I can do it for her, and I know Mr. Tuck will take out her teeth for nothing. Good-bye, dear mamma; give my love to all at home, particularly to Mary.

'Your affectionate Son,

'EDWARD BELL.

'P.S.—I forgot to say that poor Tom

Hardwick told me to remember him to you whenever I wrote. He is very well, considering, and often goes about in his hand-chair.

'P.S.—the 2nd.—I fear you will think me a very slovenly writer with my post-scripts, but I *must* tell you I had a ride on Mr. Ailsa's saddle-horse yesterday. He knows I am a good rider, so trusted me on him. It is a splendid animal, high spirited and quite thorough bred, but very gentle, and coal-black. His groom rode behind. I don't mean on the same horse. Fancy me careering past all the houses on horse-back, followed by a groom! Mr. Tuck says, when he is established he shall buy just such another steed : but he has not done walking the hospitals yet.'

'What a ridiculous letter Ned does write!' exclaimed Miss Margaret Bell, vexed that *she* was not its subject. 'Mary, you'll set yourself on fire.'

'I do not think it a ridiculous letter at all,' answered Mrs. Bell ; 'few boys of fifteen could write a better. But about this invitation to Emily? If we can manage the expense, I should like her to accept it.'

'Would the expense be very much, mamma ? ' asked Emily.

'It is the dress, you see, Emily,' answered Mrs. Bell, as she withdrew with the troublesome Mary. 'We must think about it.'

'I daresay that ancient simpleton, Miss Winnington, has some romantic notions about bringing you and your old lover, James Ailsa, together,' exclaimed Margaret, who generally managed to pick up a fund of notions herself, romantic and shrewd also.

'Don't talk so ridiculously,' retorted Emily. 'I wonder how he and poor Tom

Hardwick hit it off together now,' she mused, with a half-smile.

'You may well say "poor Tom Hardwick,"' observed Margaret, whose ill-temper was more marked than it used to be ; 'he is poor in every sense of the word. How strangely he and Ailsa seem to have changed positions ! '

'That accident was a wretched misfortune for him. I wonder, Margaret, if Tom would have ever married.'

'Married ?—no !.' returned Miss Margaret. 'It is absurd to think of it. How could he, poor as he turned out to be—how could he have thought of a wife ? After the squire died, his income scarcely allowed him to keep the man-servant who waited on him.'

'He must have entered into some means of getting money,' said Emily ; 'some profession.'

'Not he,' answered Margaret.. 'He

would have entered into debt, and so into a prison perhaps; that's what Mr. Tom Hardwick would have entered into. Nonsense! It was a strange delusion with some of you flirting girls to suppose that Tom Hardwick would ever marry.'

Emily sighed. The heart alone knoweth its own bitterness. For this man she had given up James Ailsa.

It was late on a fine spring day when the stage-coach that conveyed the passengers from the railway station to Ebury arrived at the village. Mr. Winnington and Edward Bell stepped up before it had well stopped— for Emily Bell sat there.

'Edward,' cried Mr. Winnington, 'you stay and see to the luggage—only two boxes you say, my dear. My sister is all impatience to receive you, Emily; take my old arm, child.'

The bustling surgeon stepped forwards briskly, and in a few minutes he was thundering at his door, and his sister flying to open it.

But we will pass over the meeting, and all the gossip of the evening. Emily was never tired of inquiring after old friends, or of listening to the history of the many changes that time had brought to Ebury. They kept telling her about James Ailsa: although to that subject she answered little; but she did ask about the improvements he had been making in the house and grounds.

'You will have an opportunity of judging for yourself to-morrow evening, Emily,' observed Miss Winnington, 'for we are going to take tea there.'

'But am I invited?' cried Emily, the colour rushing into her face at the recollection of how she and James had last parted.

'No, no,' laughed Miss Winnington, 'we

did not tell him you were coming : we mean to give him a surprise.'

But was it alone owing to the anticipated 'surprise' that Emily felt a tremor stealing over her when they entered Mr. Ailsa's gate the following evening? He saw their approach from the window, and stepped out to meet them.

'A young friend of ours, whom we have taken the liberty of bringing,' cried the surgeon.

It was nearly twilight, yet James Ailsa recognised her as instantly as if they had been under the sun at noonday. There was no embarrassment visible on his face; the slightest possible flush rose for a moment, and then left his features pale and placid as before. He held out his hand to her, with his own sweet smile, and welcomed her to his home.

'I thought you were to bring Edward

with you this evening,' Ailsa remarked, as they sat down to tea, which Miss Winnington made.

'No,' answered the surgeon, 'Ned is at home. He remains to run up for me in case I should be wanted. Do you know, Ailsa, I am thinking of giving up my profession.'

'Indeed!'

'The fact is, I am growing too old to do justice to my patients. Some who ought to receive a visit from me twice a day get only one; for, what with old age and rheumatism, there are times when my legs will not run over so much ground as formerly.'

'Why not take an assistant?—or partner?'

'I would take a partner to-morrow, James, but the difficulty lies in finding one to my mind. Had fortune not placed you above it, I should have tried hard to get you. Had you only come back a poor man, Ailsa!'

'I will become your partner if you wish it,' observed Ailsa quietly.

'I was speaking seriously,' returned the surgeon.

'So am I,' smiled Ailsa. 'I wish to resume my profession, and would rather do so at Ebury than anywhere else. But I never should have set up in opposition, you know.'

'You are rich enough to lead an idle life,' observed Mr. Winnington; 'why worry yourself with your profession? It has its own labour and cares, remember, James; more than some others have.'

'Well, I am not so rich as people make me out; and a medical man is never the worse for some private income, especially in a neighbourhood where the poor abound.'

'Then, my lad,' cried the old surgeon,

rising, and shaking him by the hand, 'you are my partner from this hour, and may God bless our union! Ah me, what ups and downs there are in this world! Would you believe, Emily, that Mary Hardwick, the only daughter of the proud old House of Hardwick, has had thoughts of becoming a governess.'

'A governess!' exclaimed Emily. 'She! But wherefore?'

'I will tell you. You know that, since her father's death, Mary has kept house for her brother at the Hall; and she has been in the habit, year by year, of handing over her own small income to eke out that of her brother Tom. Now the Squire's new wife is a regular skinflint, Emily, and she makes him worse than he would be; and he told Mary at Christmas last, that now she was released from her trouble with his house-keeping matters, he should not continue to

pay her personal bills, and that *she* must
discontinue that extravagant practice of
giving her own money to Tom. This set
Miss Hardwick thinking—no very pleasant
thoughts you may be sure. To withdraw
her income from Tom she was resolved
not to do; and she consulted me—poor,
humble old apothecary Winnington—about
seeking a situation as governess. The Squire
would have been up in arms, no doubt, if he
had known it : and Mary cried bitterly—
for she has a touch of the family pride, you
know.'

'And is she going out?' inquired Emily.

'No,' replied Mr. Winnington; 'and
now comes a bit of romance, Emily. A
certain sum has recently been paid into the
funds in Tom Hardwick's name, the interest
of which will nearly double his own income.
It was done in a mysterious manner; no-
one knows by whom or through whom;

but it is a godsend to Tom, who, poor fellow, has had to pinch himself at times, and will render the rest of his days comfortable. So now, you see, Mary has no scruple in withdrawing from him her own money.'

'I wonder Miss Hardwick has never married,' mused Emily.

' Why, my dear,' returned Miss Winnington, ' I do not think Mary is single for want of offers, and she has plenty of time before her yet. It is well known that she refused Lord Chiselem; and Earl Dunnely's heart, it is said, was set upon the match.'

' Who can have paid the money to assist Tom ? ' wondered Emily.

' That is a problem, perhaps never to be solved,' answered the surgeon. ' I can assure you, Emily, half the village would give their ears to know.'

So they sat talking. When they were about to leave for the night, James accompanied them to the hall-door, and there gave his arm to Emily, meaning to walk with them as far as the gates. It was a warm night, calm and still. The moon, nearly at the full, was riding along the heavens, steeping the garden before them in light. They had gone but a few paces, when Miss Winnington turned back to the house, remembering that she had left her cap behind. The surgeon followed her.

They disappeared within the hall, and Ailsa and his companion turned and waited for them. They had accidentally halted on the very spot, underneath the self-same trees where they had *last* stood together—that stormy, tempestuous night, when Ailsa stole, almost as a thief, into the grounds, to obtain one word from her; to say farewell, it might have been for ever.

'How rapidly the years have passed!'

exclaimed Emily, more in accordance with her own thoughts than in remark to him.

'Since we last met here,' he replied quickly. 'They have indeed.'

Ah, he *was* thinking of it then, even as she was.

'He told me then,' was her next thought, 'that he should strive to root me out of his heart. Did he so strive?—and did he suc-ceed?'

'Seven years!' observed Ailsa, 'seven long years! Had we known then that seven years would be the term of—of' (he seemed to hesitate for a word)—'our separation—I mean that would elapse before we met again, we should have thought it interminable; yet what is it in the retrospect?'

'What indeed!' she answered. 'It seems as a dream.'

'And it has left little mark upon us.

You, Emily, are scarcely, if at all, changed; and people tell me I am not.'

Ailsa stooped and plucked some violets, several of which grew at the foot of the trees close by, and gave them to her. 'You are fond of the scent of violets, I remember; these are very sweet ones. I wonder,' he observed, musingly, 'if they are the old roots?'

'You do not, then, quite forget all our old thoughts and feelings, our likes and dislikes,' she said, with apparent calmness, but with a beating heart.

'Not quite,' he quietly replied.

'How stupid of you both to stand stock still!' broke out the surgeon, advancing with Miss Winnington; 'I told you to walk on. And you without your hat, James!'

'What a lovely night it is!' exclaimed Emily to Ailsa. 'Everything seems so still, so full of peace.'

'Yes,' he replied, 'it serves as a contrast to the one when we were last here together. The elements were jarring enough then.'

'Ah, that was a wretched night. You did not take cold, I hope, James? I thought at the time you inevitably would do so.'

'Take—what did you say?' He seemed lost in thought.

'Cold.'

'Cold? Oh no, I think not. If I did, I don't remember it now; and I am sure I did not heed it then.'

Ailsa wished them good-night when they reached the gate, and turned to retrace his steps indoors. 'The night is beautiful indeed, as she said,' he repeated to himself, 'and is a contrast to *that* one. They seem a type of my fortunes: then they were as the weather—black, stormy, and apparently

without hope; now they are bright as this
lovely scene. Oh, the misery, the misery of
that night! And yet, anguish as it was to
me, all that dark period of my existence, I
would afterwards have given my opening
prospects to live it over again—to exchange
for it the terrible apathy to all human
things which alone it left me. Why, why
should we be in such haste to love?—why
hasten to wear away the fresh green of the
tree of life only that we may sear it for
ever?'

'She is altered for the better,' he resumed after a while, 'for she is more quiet
and subdued. I do not think she would
flirt so much now,' he continued, with a
melancholy smile, 'even with Mr. Tom
Hardwick, were he the gay gallant he used
to be. Fallen circumstances and seven years
have worked their traces upon her mind,
though they may have spared her counte-

nance. And for me?—the romance of life passed away with her: I must see what I can make of the reality.'

'Are Mr. Ailsa and Tom Hardwick friends now?' inquired Emily as they walked home, putting the question with indifference.

'Very good friends indeed,' answered the surgeon. 'Excellent friends. Ailsa often calls at his lodgings, and chats with him, to pass away one of his many weary hours. Poor Tom! they hang heavily upon his hands.'

Fifty times that night did Emily ask herself if Ailsa still loved her. He had met her cordially; he had voluntarily given her his arm to the outer gates, and had conversed with her, though slightly, upon former days; he had plucked violets for her, remembering that she was partial to them—in all this, was there, or was there not, a lurking sentiment of love? 'Time alone must prove,' sighed Emily.

But time seemed to prove nothing. Eight or ten weeks elapsed, and things remained just as they were then. She saw Ailsa frequently. His manner to her was always friendly, but he had not again alluded to bygone days. Emily went to the Hall, and was introduced to its new mistress. She did not like her; few did; but sweet Mary Hardwick, kind and considerate as ever, served to compensate for the austere character of her sister-in-law.

She was invited to the Hall, to one of their formal dinner-parties; when the side-boards groaned with plate, and the servants were so numerous that they trod on each other's heels. Emily could not help thinking how much better it would be, if some of the silver and domestics had been disposed of, and the proceeds applied to enlarge Tom's income : if he did not want it now, he *had* wanted it. But near in some matters as the Squire was, it would have broken his heart to diminish the old baronial state, which custom, and their own ideas, had rendered indispensable to the head of the House of Hardwick. Ailsa was there also that evening : he seemed to be a favoured and frequent visitor.

III.

INVITATIONS went out from James Ailsa for a sort of rustic fête; a house-warming he called it to Miss Winnington. Young ladies as well as old were invited; many; and people laughingly said he meant to choose a wife at it. Emily Bell's pulses beat as she heard it.

Would *she* be his choice? The doubt was of too weighty a moment to her to be idly guessed at. She loved Ailsa now. Formerly, when her attention had been distracted by others, Emily had loved him in her own fashion, and perhaps almost as much as she was capable of loving anyone. But the last few weeks, when she had been led into daily contact with him—

listened to his voice, leaned upon his arm—
had brought, indeed, a passion to her heart
deeper than of old. Yet Ailsa had not *now*
striven to plant it there : not a word or a
look had escaped him that might not have
been given—say—to old Miss Winnington.

The day brought weather with it warm
and lovely. Dancing on the lawn was one of
the amusements. Ailsa had stood up twice
only, once with Miss Hardwick, the second
time with Emily. Was it for the abstract
pleasure of dancing with her that he had
singled her out for the honour, when so
many were present, who, from their rank
and position, might be considered as having
a better right to it ; or was he desirous to
show to the world that he did not slight one
who, it was pretty generally believed, had
once held the first place in his heart ?

The evening was growing dusk, and the
sound of the music and dancing was still

heard, but Ailsa was not joining in it. He was strolling in a distant part of the grounds—the reader may see him there, with a young lady by his side, and may listen to what he is saying.

'When, Mary, are my days of probation to end? They have endured these several weeks, and had I not guessed the reason of their being imposed, I should have borne them less patiently.'

She looked up quickly; and as she met his eyes fixed upon hers, and saw the half-saucy, half-tender smile upon his countenance, some of the proud Hardwick blood rushed to her face.

'James,' she faltered, 'what do you mean?'

'Before you gave the irrevocable promise to be mine,' he said, gliding his arm round her waist, 'you were willing to ascertain if any remains of my love for Miss Bell still lingered, or if it would break out again. You need not have doubted me, Mary.'

'Pray forgive me,' she said, bursting into tears.

'My dear love, there is nothing to forgive,' he answered. 'Had you only given me a hint, I should have spoken then as I am about to speak now; as I always intended to speak before we married. Now listen to me, Mary,' and he drew her closer to him as they walked. 'You suspect that I once loved Emily Bell. I did indeed love her; none can know how passionately, or picture the bitter anguish that overwhelmed me when I awoke to reality. Life and its events; the world and its hopes and cares; the present, past, future—all seemed to me a blank: a long, dark, dreamy blank it appears to me now when I look back upon it. But I struggled hard to overcome this, I struggled hard to forget her, and I succeeded *in time* ; and so effectually, that no trace of love or liking for her is left. I look at her now, and can scarcely believe she is the girl I was once so infatuated with : so our feelings change. I tell you this,' he proceeded, ' for you have a right now to know every hidden thought and feeling of mine ; but believe me, Mary, you will not find that your husband will cherish you less, because you were not his first love.'

' I do believe you,' she whispered.

' I cannot promise to love you,' he resumed, ' with the same infatuated passion that I bore for her, neither would it be well, for either of us, Mary ; for, rely upon it, that dream of Elysium is only meant for the short romance of early youth ; it could not long survive marriage and the realities of later life. And where such love does fall, *and end,* as end it must, it shatters almost unto death.'

'You left Ebury, I believe, because some-one interfered between you?' asked Miss Hardwick.

'Yes. I knew then that she did not return my love, that she was only playing with me for her own amusement. I had suspected it at times, but I only knew it positively the very night before I left—the night preceding the steeplechase. And if she had given me, that night, but one word of *hope*, one word of love, Mary, I should have returned now to claim her; and *we* should never have been to each other but strangers. At that interview the conviction was forced upon me that she was a vain, deceitful, and heartless girl.'

'I always thought—though believe me, James, I say this in no spirit of rivalry—that she was not worthy of you.'

'I think so now, Mary. Or, rather—for you will say that admission savours of egregious vanity—I think she was very unsuited to me.'

' It was said at the time that it was my brother Tom who interfered between you, and caused the separation.'

' You shall know as much of the matter one day as I do. Unless,' he proceeded in a tone of inexpressible tenderness, ' unless you will fear to consign your happiness— that of a whole life, Mary—to the keeping of one who has been bold enough to make the hazardous confession that he cannot love you as he once loved another ? '

But Ailsa knew the question to be un- necessary as he spoke.

' James,' resumed Miss Hardwick after a pause, ' you say we are not to have any secrets from each other, as I trust we never shall have—but I think you have still kept one from me. The unknown benefactor of my brother Tom ; who has made the re-

mainder of his days easy; that friend was
—yourself.'

Ailsa remained silent; but the tell-tale
blood rushed to his face.

'Am I not right? You will surely trust
me.'

'You are right, Mary,' he replied.
' But, I pray you, let not a word of this
pass your lips.'

' As you will,' she said. 'I wish I could,
in his name, thank you for it as I ought.'

' You can do that by never mentioning
the subject.'

'What could have been your motive?'
she continued. 'It is rare that one confers
such benefit on an enemy, and in that light
I believe you once regarded Tom, perhaps
with cause.'

' *I had a motive*,' replied Ailsa solemnly,
' but I shall never explain it to you in all
its details.'

'Some time,' was her remark. 'There must come a day for full confidence between us.'

'In all else, Mary, but not in this; even when you shall be my wife. But I will give you the outline at once, and then please let the matter drop between us for ever. I thought ill of your brother; *I wished him ill;* and though it is quite impossible my sinful wish could have brought the evil upon him, yet—but—that is all, Mary.'

'But Tom did not know you wished him ill?'

'No human being heard it or knew it. It lay between myself and God.'

'How seriously you speak, James!' she exclaimed, looking earnestly at him.

'My love, let us forget the subject; it is extremely painful to me.' He turned as he spoke, and they proceeded in the direction of the lights and the crowd.

They were beginning to let off the fireworks, when Ailsa ran into the house to see
that none of his guests remained indoors,
but in the little room opening to the greenhouse he found Miss Winnington.

'Make haste and come with me,' he said ;
'I will find you a place.'

'I would not stir out for all the fireworks
in the three kingdoms, James, and you into
the bargain,' rejoined the old lady. 'No
standing in the night air for me, since I
had rheumatic fever. I shall remain where
I am. But one word, James, before
you go. What is this report that is being
whispered? People say you are about to
marry.'

'And for once people say right.'

'Upon whom has your choice fallen?
Upon Emily?'

'No, no. Cannot you make a better
guess?'

Miss Winnington clasped her hands. 'Oh, James!'

'Are you displeased at my choice—do you not approve it?'

'I have no right to be displeased at it, and none could disapprove of Mary Hardwick. You see I have guessed. But—I must speak out, James—I thought you were once so fervently attached to Emily Bell.'

'So I was; passionately attached to her.'

'And I deemed that if any one's love could have withstood the shocks of time, it was yours.'

'Time did not change my love,' he answered, with a shade of agitation in his voice; '*she* changed it.'

'Alas! I have sometimes feared so. And my little dream of romance is over.'

'It is. But my dear, long-tried friend, I have seen and thanked you for it. You thought to serve two hearts by bringing her hither; to unite those upon whom the ban of separation had been forced. Had that separation alone stood between them, you would have been rewarded; but I am not the less grateful for the kindness.'

'You have no love left for her, then?'

'None; or worse than none. There is not a young lady here to-night that I would not choose for my wife in preference to her. I do not know why this feeling should exist; I only know that it does, and that I cannot avoid or mitigate it.'

'Do you think she has so completely for-gotten you?'

Ailsa quite laughed. 'The task for her could not have been a difficult one. She never cared for me.'

Ailsa left by one door, and Miss Win-nington pushed open the other, which was ajar. But in passing into the greenhouse, she almost stumbled over Emily.

'Why—Emily! How came you here? Did you hear my conversation with James Ailsa?'

She burst into tears, and threw herself into the old lady's arms as she spoke. 'I heard it all—all; but not intentionally. I came into the greenhouse, and some one, when I would have gone out, had fastened the door upon me; Ned, perhaps, for mischief. I could not come out this way and betray to you both that I was here.'

'My poor girl!' breathed Miss Winnington, for she saw how deeply Emily's feelings had been shaken.

'Oh, that wicked propensity for flirtation!' exclaimed the excited girl; 'had I never given way to it, and neglected him, whom I really loved, for others, how different it would have been now!'

'Ah, my dear, to tell the truth, I always blamed you. Few persons have the opportunity given them of attaching a heart such as Ailsa's. But you were attracted, girl-like, by the gay plumage of Mr. Tom Hard-wick, and other such worthless butterflies. Let it be a warning to you, my child.'

'The warning has come too late,' sighed Emily, pressing her hands upon her aching brow. 'Would I had never returned here, for it has taken away all my hope in life.'

'You must not take things too much to heart,' cried Miss Winnington, using, un-consciously, almost the very words that had once been spoken by Emily to Ailsa.

'There's a bright firework!' exclaimed Emily, dropping her hands from her tem-ples, and changing her tone. 'I shall go and see them.'

As she quitted the hall-door, she encoun-tered Ailsa. He expressed his surprise that she was not where everyone else was, and turned to conduct her.

'I went into the house to see Miss Winnington,' panted Emily; 'her cold is bad, and she will not come out.'

'How did you go in, then? I have been standing here, and did not see you.'

'I went through the greenhouse, but some one locked it after me, so I could not return that way.'

'I fastened the greenhouse,' he said. 'Upon seeing the door open, I thought it safer that it should be kept shut, lest some sparks should get in and injure the plants. But that is not very recently. You must have been in some time, Emily.'

Their eyes met; and, for a moment, neither withdrew the gaze. He saw that his conversation with Miss Winnington had been heard, and she felt that he saw it. She released his arm, and murmuring something about the fireworks darted away, like a fawn, across the grass. Had she stood one minute longer, she would have fallen into hysterics, and sobbed upon his breast, as she had done that stormy, never-to-be-forgotten night.

IV.

THE day came at last on which Emily was to depart from Ebury. Had she followed her own inclinations, she would have left when she first heard of James Ailsa's engagement; but Miss Winnington would not permit this. It was somewhat singular, though quite the result of accident, that her departure was fixed for the same day as the marriage.

'Farewell, farewell, dear Miss Winnington,' she said, tears running down her cheeks, ' and thank you for all your kindness.'

'Take care how you get in, Emily,' exclaimed the surgeon, as they reached the coach; 'another step. Oh, you need not laugh, Mr. Edward; young legs make light of such matters, but old ones like mine feel that bruises are easier got than cured. You are sure you have everything, my dear? Don't forget that you have promised us another visit next summer; we shall not fail to claim it.'

She shook hands with Mr. Winnington, and bent down to kiss her brother.

'Be a good boy, Edward,' she whispered, 'and do all you can to serve Mr. and Miss Winnington, in return for their great kindness to you.'

'I will, Emily, I will indeed,' answered the boy; 'you may tell mamma so.'

'All right,' cried Mr. Winnington, as he closed the door with a bang. And the coach rolled onwards.

Emily remained lost in thought till they came near the Hall, when, aware of the festivities which had that morning taken place, she leaned forward and looked from the window.

They were close upon the lodge gates, when the coach took a sudden swerve, to give place to a chariot-and-four which was bowling through them, on its way from the Hall, in the old-fashioned style of the day. It contained James Ailsa and his bride.

Before Emily was prepared for this, her glance had encountered theirs. She bowed to them, quite unconscious at the moment of what she did, and they both returned it. A crimson blush overspread Mary's face, but *his* remained perfectly calm. It needed not this to convince Emily how completely he had forgotten her.

It was but a momentary meeting. Almost as Emily looked, the carriage had passed, leaving its cloud of dust behind. The stage-coachman, after an admiring eye given to the lost equipage, whipped up his horses to gain the station in time for the half-past two o'clock train; and Emily Bell, sinking into the darkest corner of the empty coach, sobbed bitterly.

THE END.

C & G.

PRINTED BY
SPOTTISWOODE AND CO., NEW-STREET SQUARE
LONDON

www.ingramcontent.com/pod-product-compliance
Lightning Source LLC
Chambersburg PA
CBHW020901020726

47497CB00005B/1507